WINGER

A SEATTLE SHARKS NOVEL

SAMANTHA WHISKEY

ALSO BY SAMANTHA WHISKEY

The Seattle Sharks Series:

Grinder

Enforcer

A Modern-Day Fairytale Romance:

The Crown

(Sneak Peek at the end of Winger!)

The Throne

To anyone who needs encouragement—you are enough.
You'll always be enough.

PROLOGUE

JEANNINE

Six Months Ago

The shot of Patron slid down my throat like water, but the buzz in my head told me I'd had three.

"Fuck yes!" I cheered, slamming the glass down on the bar. "Another!"

"I'm with her," Warren said, clinking his own shot glass against the bar. He sat so close his muscled arm brushed against mine, and my insides purred.

"How'd we get stuck together?" I teased, taking the next round of Patron from the bartender.

"Our friends are all stupid in love with each other."

I snapped my fingers, nodding. "That's right." I threw the shot back, hissing slightly. "I've never seen my girls happier."

"Same for Gage and Rory," Warren said after he'd taken his own shot. He rubbed at the scruff on his chiseled chin as he scanned the crowd for our friends. He smiled at them across the room, then spun around to face me.

"You next?" I asked, motioning for another shot.

He cocked an eyebrow at me, those dark eyes just a bit glazed from the liquor. "Next for what?"

"Getting hitched?" I chuckled. "Seems like the Sharks are on a hot streak."

They'd won the Stanley Cup.

Gage and Bailey had an eight-month-old son.

Rory and Paige had a four-month-old baby girl.

Odds were Warren was next, cause it sure as hell wasn't going to be me.

Warren laughed. "Hell no. The Sharks are on a hot streak because I'm focused on the ice—my career. But we'll see how this season goes without me."

"Right!" We were there celebrating his going away since he was taking this season off to play for Canada in the Olympics. He'd worked that out in contract negotiation since the NHL wasn't pausing the season for the games this round.

"I don't have time for a relationship, let alone a wife," he continued, and I nodded.

"That's how I am with my restaurants. I've put in way too much of my time to throw it all away to be someone's homemaker." I chuckled, and he handed me my next shot.

"To not getting married."

We clinked our glasses together and threw the contents back.

My insides were on fire in the best way, my muscles loose. God, I'd needed this night off. I'd have to thank Bailey for that later—the babies were with the Grandmas—and she'd dragged us all out to celebrate Warren's going away.

I glanced over my shoulder, watching her as she was practically attached to Gage across the room.

Maybe much later. I grinned at her before returning focus to the beast of a man next to me.

Hot *damn* he was glorious.

Tall, ripped, with slightly shaggy black hair, dark eyes, chiseled features, and cocky to boot.

If I had wanted to roll around with a man more than once, it'd be someone like him. Not that I *had* gotten a chance to see what Warren Kinley was made of...but now that I was thinking about it, I sort of couldn't *not* think about it.

My core purred again, and I wetted my lips.

I hadn't had sex in months—thanks to being married to my job.

Tonight was my first night off in just as many.

"What about kids?" I asked, wanting to keep him talking. Keep him sitting next to me.

"You're joking, right?"

I shrugged. "Just because marriage is out of the question doesn't mean kids are. Look at Gage." He'd had Lettie before Bailey and him were an item, and she was one of the most amazing little girls I'd ever met.

Warren nodded, motioning for another round of shots.

"Truth," he said. "Gage somehow can manage both—being an awesome father and a star on the ice. Me? I'm not that multi-talented." He handed me another shot. "I'd be a shit dad. Always on the road for games. More worried about the ice and the opponents than diaper changes and the Disney Channel."

I clinked his glass. "It's nice being on the same page."

I threw the shot back, my heart fluttering from the buzz

and the delicious smell of Warren—crisp, spicy, and a hint of salt. Almost more intoxicating than the tequila.

"No little ones on the brain?" He asked.

"Nope." I made sure my lips popped on the word, drawing his attention there. I smiled when his eyes trailed back up to my eyes. "I'm content being a surrogate aunt to Ethan, Daphne, and Lettie," I said. "They easily satisfy any rare moments I contemplate motherhood."

"You're pretty damn incredible—you know that?" He asked, leaning forward.

I reached up and boldly touched the scruff on his chin—our nearly year-long flirt fest giving me the confidence to do so.

"Oh, honey, you have no idea," I said, enjoying the prickly sensation on the pads of my fingers.

"Is that right?" He cocked an eyebrow and damn if my stomach didn't flip.

"You want to find out?" I let go of his chin, standing up enough to brush my chest against his.

So I was being forward.

So I might be desperate for a good orgasm fest.

At least Warren knew where I stood and I knew his terms, too.

It was simply a bonus he was the hottest Shark on the team, not that I'd ever tell that to Bailey or Paige.

"Fuck yes," he whispered, mimicking my earlier words to the delicious bottle of Patron.

"Then let's get out of here," I said, reaching for his hand and leading the way through the packed crowd. His fingers were strong and warm, interlocked between mine as I made my way to the parking lot. The cool breeze shook off some of the alcohol, and I spun around, slipping slightly into his ridiculously muscled chest. "You have a driver like the rest of the Sharks, right?"

He smirked and waved his free hand. A few minutes later, a big black SUV rolled to a stop in front of us.

"Hockey stardom has perks," I said, stepping into the car as he held the door open for me.

"Oh, honey, you have no idea," he echoed my earlier words and a warm shiver trailed right down my spine. "Your place or mine?" He asked after he'd buckled his seatbelt.

"Mine is closer," I said and gave the driver my address.

Warren held my hand the entire ten-minute drive to my apartment. He traced his fingers over the creases, my knuckles, the soft part of my wrist, the trail igniting my blood. He was gentle, teasing, and it made me ache between the thighs. If this innocent touch could get me wet, I couldn't wait to see what he could do to me once we were inside.

I hurried up the stairs, totally grateful—I was well-practiced in climbing the things in my stilettos. I didn't slip once.

Gold star for me.

"You in a rush?" He asked, taking his sweet ass time climbing the stairs as I stood there holding my front door open for him.

"We've been dancing around each other for over a year," I said, never one to beat around the bush. "And you're about to disappear for six months. Can you blame me?" I asked, raking my eyes up and down his gorgeous frame.

The man had his damned suit jacket slung over one shoulder, the white button down underneath tight over his muscles. And that smirk that shaped his lips?

Fuck me.

Yes please.

He stopped within an inch of me, his hand on my hip as he

pressed his body to mine, my spine against my door. He traced the edge of my jaw with his nose and inhaled deeply. After my eyes had properly rolled back in my head, he pulled away.

"God, you smell good," he said before turning into my apartment.

I took two steps inside and locked the door behind me.

Butterflies flapped in my stomach, my breath tight in my lungs as I watched him check out my place.

It took me a minute to figure out why my breath came in short, anxious bursts.

For the first time since before I could remember, I was *nervous*.

I didn't get nervous.

I ate men like him for breakfast.

So why am I trembling?

I tossed my purse and keys on my wooden drop station by the door and clicked over to him with shaking knees.

Maybe it was because I *knew* him.

We were friends—our best friends being married kind of forced it.

This is why I usually stick to strangers. Can't be nervous when you don't know the guy.

Warren laid his jacket on my desk that sat across from my giant kitchen—the sole reason I rented this place. The kitchen was almost as good as the one at my restaurant.

Small closet, big stove.

Compromise for perfection.

"Come here," he said, flicking his fingers at me in a come-hither motion.

Normally I'd fly off at the mouth—make the man come to me—but there was something about

Warren that made me *obey*.

Something powerful and irresistible.

And after shamelessly flirting for over a year, I was more than ready to see what he could do.

Instead of going straight for my ass like I assumed the beast of a man would, he cupped my face in his hands. Inching his lips downward, he took an eternity to barely brush them over mine.

The man liked the tease, the anticipation.

It made me breathless.

I fingered the back of his black hair, gripping it as he finally crushed his lips on mine.

I moaned into his mouth when his tongue slid over the edges of my teeth. He rubbed and lapped and claimed my mouth with expert flicks and sucks.

Hot damn, I was churning between my thighs from just a kiss.

I pressed back with all I had, hooking my leg around his hip, sighing when I felt the pressure of his rock hard cock through his dress pants. I rolled my hips, needing the pressure, the friction, so badly I hadn't realized how much.

Note to self: never let it go this long between shags again. You end up dry humping a Shark.

I laughed at my absurdity, and he jerked back.

"What is funny?" There was a mischievous spark in his dark eyes.

"Ohmygod, not you," I said, realizing how that sounded. "*Me*. It's been too long. I really need this."

He gripped my hips, jerking me harder against him. "Then that makes two of us."

He kissed me again, hard yet sweet...like the best candy.

If I wasn't careful I might get hooked on that kiss.

I drew back, my heels clicking against the hardwood as I swished my hips toward my bedroom. I shed a piece of clothing as I went, happy when I glanced behind me to find him doing the same. By the time I stood at the foot of my bed, I was in my stilettos, a purple lace thong, and a matching bralette.

He was in—

"Holy hell," I said, gasping at the sight of him.

"Don't act so surprised," he said, stepping toward me in nothing but a sleek pair of black briefs. He slipped his fingers into my long blonde hair. "Don't pretend like you and the girls haven't Googled our calendar shoot."

I smacked his ass as hard as I could, enjoying the hiss that came from his lips and the flames that flickered in his eyes.

"I knew you were cocky," I said and glanced at his considerable length beneath the fabric, just because I could. "But I guess I didn't realize just *how* much."

He flicked his tongue over my lips, then moved lower as he palmed my breasts. Every nerve in my body stood at attention, the sensation rippling over my skin like a warm chill.

"No strings," he said, sucking my hard nipple over the lace. "Right?" He glanced up at me as he kissed his way lower, over my tummy and down...

"Did you already forget our conversation at the bar?" I asked, breathless. "Have you not paid attention to how I behave this whole time our friends have been together?"

"Oh, I've paid plenty of attention," he said. "Trust me, Nine. You're a hard woman to ignore." His hot breath washed over the lace covering my center. And my knees about buckled from the sight of this massive man on his knees before me. "Still," he continued as his stubble teased the inside of my thighs. "I need to know for certain. Our friends are our family. We're friends, too. So...no strings?" he asked again.

"None," I hissed, arching as he teased me over the lace. "You know that."

"Can never be too be sure." He smiled up at me. "I can't have you falling in love with me."

"Not a chance, Warren." I laughed, scraping my nails over his scalp. "I'm not the falling type."

He gripped the hem of my lace and tugged it over my thighs until I stepped out of the fabric. His eyes widened, lust churning in the darkness of his eyes as he took in every bare inch of me.

"Fuck," he hissed. "Then you may just be the perfect woman."

"Hey, now, this works both ways." I tsked him. "You can't fall for me, either."

"I won't," he said.

"Promise?" I asked, holding on to his hair.

"Promise," he said and then slipped his tongue between my thighs.

I arched my head back, thankful he had a good hold of my ass because I was ready to fall backward.

Good God, the Shark knew how to use his tongue.

Not surprising with him being the last active member of the once bad boy trio.

He lapped and sucked and hummed and worked his fingers into the dance too.

"Oh. My. God." I moaned, that hot livewire down my center yanking taut. "Warren, fuck."

"Mmm," he moaned against me, and my stomach swirled and tightened. "I fucking love your dirty mouth." He didn't back away as he spoke and the vibrations made me tremble.

"Mmm," I copied him. "I fucking love your tongue."

"God damn, woman." He slipped two fingers inside me,

and I arched into his mouth, needing more of him on me, inside me.

He complied, sucking on my clit as he pumped those fingers until I was a coiled spring ready to burst on his tongue.

"Yes!" I screamed as I shattered, the hot, tight energy spiraling down the center of me in sparkling bursts.

My entire body released one hell of a sigh.

Damn it had been way too long since I'd had one that big.

Hell, I may never have had one that big.

Warren trailed kisses upward, finally towering over me again. He chuckled, flashing me a sexy-as-sin smirk that had no doubt aided him in dropping countless panties.

The bad-boy status only made me want him more—someone to keep up with my practically insatiable appetite.

And for just tonight?

He was *mine*.

For the next twelve hours.

I flashed him a look that promised I'd put him to work.

He shot me one back that promised he never backed away from a challenge.

Good. We already have the silent communication down.

To be fair, we'd been eye-fucking each other for months. I'm shocked his kiss alone hadn't made me come.

In one quick swoop, I was on my back, my bed catching my fall.

"Stay," he said, snapping his fingers as he went in search of something. He came back a few seconds later with a foil packet in his hand.

He slipped off his briefs and went to rip open the packet.

"Nuh-uh," I said, shaking my head. I propped myself up

on my elbows and gazed at his beautiful body, from the carved from wood abs to the insanely strong arms that could toss me around like a doll to the damn-near perfect, rock-hard cock. "You think I'm wasting that with a condom?"

He tilted his head. "I thought we agreed neither of us is next in line for a baby."

"Exactly why I'm on birth control of the highest kind." I winked at him. "And I'm totally clean. If you want to be triple safe, I get it. But if you want to *feel* me…" I shifted so my legs were parted, revealing what he'd just made swollen and aching for him. "Then come here."

"What about me? Aren't you worried I might—"

"You act like I don't know you, Warren," I said, chuckling. "We've run in the same circle for over a year now. I know you. I know you're smart, clean."

He pursed his lips, a small battle raging in his eyes. It only took a few seconds before he tossed the packet over his shoulder and jumped on the bed.

"Oh, thank God," I said, kissing him hard as he settled between my thighs. I ran my fingers over every gloriously muscled inch of him, wondering how in the hell I'd resisted this urge for so long. "I was worried you'd be a closet boy scout."

"Me?" He pressed the tip of his cock against the apex of my thighs, and I hissed. "Just took me a minute to realize you were right."

"I'm always right," I said, nipping at his bottom lip as I arched my hips upward, trying to take him in.

He kept away enough to torture me.

"Greedy woman," he teased.

"Boy scout," I challenged.

He growled and pinned both my hands above my head with one of his. The other was busy spreading my thighs as wide as they could possibly go. His eyes trailed the length of my body, hungry in their gaze.

"I'm not sure if you're ready for this," he said, teasing my wetness with his fingers.

"Oh, I'm more than ready. Hit me with your best shot, Shark."

He smirked before slamming his lips down on mine. I took his tongue in my mouth, claiming him as easily as he claimed me. He may be used to the submissive puck bunny type, but I was here to *play*.

Just like him.

We were the same.

Wanted the same things.

Our careers.

And one wild night between the sheets.

He jerked his head back, those dark eyes churning.

"You asked for it," he said before thrusting.

Nothing about this man was gentle—he was all hard edges, rough scruff, and pure, undiluted man.

Such a rare treat to have someone so confident between my legs.

"Yes," I said, moaning as his length filled me.

Damn, he was *huge*.

I hadn't expected less from the beast of a man.

My walls were snug around him despite being slippery from his mouth. He kept my hands pinned even though I pushed against them, wanting to claw my nails into his back.

"Fucking perfect," he growled as he thrust again and again, his free hand pressing one of my thighs to the bed so he could pump deeper. "I can feel every delicious inch of you."

He filled me, over and over, the angle hitting every

single hot-spot I possessed and coiling that sweet tension within me again.

I never once shut my eyes, content to watch him take control of my body and make it sing for him.

I melted between his thrusts, clenched around him with each expertly timed roll of my hips.

He was glorious to look at—all hard ridges and smooth skin and pure strength.

Damn, this man was everything.

The perfect combination of safe and sin.

He moved his hand from my thigh to my clit, rolling it with just the right amount of pressure to make me scream.

"Fuck," he hissed as I clenched hard around him.

I reached up, claiming his mouth as I came, needing to feel him inside me in every way possible.

A deep shudder ran through him, and he found his release inside me but never broke our kiss.

Slowly, he worked us both down until our hungry, greedy kisses and touches turned into soft, sweet, feather-light caresses.

After a few moments, he rolled over, crashing on his back. "*Damn.*"

"Damn," I agreed.

It had been too long, that was true...but I'd never had a ride like that before.

He turned his head to look at me. "Do I need to leave right this second or..."

I smiled. "I don't have an early meeting if you don't."

"I don't," he said quickly. "I don't have to be at the airport until five tomorrow evening."

"Then stay?" I bit my bottom lip. "And we can say goodbye after a morning session?"

The smile that shaped his lips *actually* made my heart skip.

Damn.

The man was too good in bed. He was confusing the hell out of my body.

"Sounds perfect," he said, settling into my bed. "How could I resist another taste?" He reached down between us, lazily tracing the lines of my hand again.

Heat crashed over my skin from the light touch, and it took all the strength I had to not move his hand to where I was already aching and ready for him again.

My girls hadn't lied.

Swimming with Sharks was the only way to go.

CHAPTER 1

JEANNINE

PRESENT DAY

"I can't believe you've kept it from us this long," Paige scolded me as I waddled around my apartment, mocktails in hand.

I gave her one, then Bailey.

"I can't believe we're still talking about this," I said, swallowing the lump in my throat.

I loved them, and I knew they meant well, but they didn't know what it was like to be *me* in this situation.

For them, babies had *always* been in their future.

For me? They'd *never* been part of the plan.

One hot night six months ago had blown my *career-only* future to hell.

At first, I'd been terrified.

Then angry.

Then in denial.

It had taken me three months to actually tell the girls I

was pregnant, and I swore them to secrecy—they couldn't tell the guys.

I still hadn't told them who the father was.

It was easy enough for them to not be able to guess—I was a party girl on my seldom nights off—or I *used to be*.

Bailey sipped her mocktail. "You know we love you no matter who it is, right?"

I sighed, hiding behind my drink.

"Yes," I finally said. "I don't know why this has to be the topic of every girl's night we have."

"Because we know how hard it is to do this on your own!" Paige said, likely thinking of Daphne—who was now ten months old and certainly bossing Rory around right this second.

"Exactly," Bailey agreed. Gage had Lettie and Ethan solo tonight, giving us this rare and much needed-girls' night. "And we want you to have all the support you need. Maybe if you told the father—"

"I *did*!" I took a deep breath, absently rubbing my hand over my belly.

I was lucky to be tall—even at six months pregnant, eating everything in sight—I still had my legs and my boobs. It only looked like I'd swallowed a basketball.

"What?" They both said at the same time.

"Yeah," I said, sipping my drink. "I left him a message."

"A message?" Again, they chided me at the same time.

"If you two keep this up I'm going to kick you both out."

They shared a concerned glance, then after a silent conversation I heard all too well, Bailey took the floor. "You have to try harder than that, Jeannine."

"Why?" I whined. "Honestly, I *know* the guy. He never wanted kids. Hell, he never wanted a relationship. I'm not going to subject this kid to that kind of rejection just because my birth control decided to fail during..." I stopped myself before I could say *the hottest sex of my life.*

Maybe that is why I'd gotten pregnant.

Maybe Warren's seed was too strong or some shit.

Or maybe you did something wrong: like take it an hour late or early or God knows what.

I still didn't have an answer, and maybe I never would.

I'd decided months ago that it didn't matter.

That obviously this baby was *meant* to be mine and mine alone.

Warren never wanted this.

Still stung that he never returned that message.

"Jeannine," Bailey said, almost cooing.

She was really too good a friend to me.

Both of them were.

The second I told them, they'd done nothing but support every decision I'd made since—even the time when I put crushed Cheetos on my chocolate ice-cream. I was a chef for Christ's sake, pregnant or not that was a bad choice.

It didn't help that the guys were supportive, too, even if they didn't know what was going on. They thought my absence around them was due to me trying to get the green-light for a fourth location. Still, they offered this family dynamic where anything I needed was only a phone call away. I was damn lucky, but it also was hard as hell to know Gage and Rory were around, and Warren wasn't.

Missed an entire season because he was off being some Olympic athlete bull shit.

Hello bitter.

I took a deep breath. Even though I knew he didn't want this, I at least wanted him to *know* this baby was his, too. But that *I* had everything under control. I didn't need his money or even his time.

Then what do I want?

That was the question.

"I want to be a good mom," I said out loud.

"You will be," Paige said.

"You'll be the best mom," Bailey agreed. "And we know you will be whether you tell this guy or not."

"I told you, I left a message." I tried not to growl.

I was hot and hormonal and just so tired of thinking about Warren. Our night haunted me in more ways than one—that whole rumor about getting hornier in the second trimester? Totally fucking true. I couldn't reach myself to get off properly, and I'd sworn off men for the next eighteen years.

"Come on, Jeannine," Paige snapped. "You are a strong, self-sustaining, bad-ass chef, and an incredible woman. We know you don't need the man. We're not asking you to throw an engagement party. But he deserves more than a message. And you owe it to yourself to know for sure what his move is in this or not."

I sighed.

I knew they were right.

But I was ignoring it.

I could do that, right? Pregnancy card and all.

"Ohmygod," Bailey said, her eyes widening as she stared at my belly.

"What?" I jolted, slamming my drink down and rubbing my hands all over my belly as she continued to stare.

"What the hell, Bailey?" Paige asked.

"You said *party*," she whispered, glancing at Paige then to me.

My heart stopped and restarted in my chest.

They couldn't know.

If they knew, they'd find a way to force Warren and me into a room.

They were married to his best friends. They had power like that.

"So?" Paige waved her hand in a *get to the point* motion.

"The last party we threw—Warren's going away—was *six* months ago."

"Who wants another drink?" I asked, forcing myself out of the chair and rushing toward the kitchen.

The girls followed me, Bailey looking shocked, and Paige looking clueless.

Damn you, Bailey.

"She's six months pregnant." Bailey rested her hands on my kitchen island.

Paige gasped. "So, the father was at Warren's party?"

I closed my eyes.

"Who would she sleep with at—" Paige's words died as she clamped her hands over her mouth.

Damn you, both.

I smoothed my hand over my stomach, the life inside me flipping around as my heart rate spiked.

It always did whenever I thought about actually facing Warren.

Seeing him after all these months.

So much had changed.

I had changed.

And not just my body, but my outlook. What I used to believe would be a damper on my career was now a much-anticipated hope and thrill inside me.

I was going to be a mom.

This baby was mine.

My heart.

My soul.

And I couldn't wait to take care of him or her.

But if Warren knew—there was a possibility he might want to rob me of this solo-mission I'd taken upon myself. And he said it himself; he'd be a terrible father. I wasn't about to let my baby be subjected to that.

"Jeannine," Bailey said, somehow her quiet voice so damned loud in the silent kitchen. "Why didn't you tell us?"

"He doesn't want a baby." I shrugged. "He didn't want any of this."

"Gage has talked to him like a dozen times in the last six months!"

"Rory, too," Paige added.

I pinched the bridge of my nose. "I know," I said. "Back when I wasn't showing I was there for some of those times. Aren't you wondering why Gage and Rory haven't brought *this* up?" I pointed to my stomach. "Why they still don't know about me?"

They both blinked at me.

"Because Warren *hasn't* talked to them about it. Never brought it up." I sighed. "I left him a message. He chose to ignore it. Case closed."

Bailey shook her head. "Warren may be a beast-like playboy, but he isn't a bad guy. He wouldn't ignore this."

"He really wouldn't," Paige said, her hand on my shoulder.

"Well," I said, a dark chuckle on my lips. "He sure has a funny way of showing attention, then."

"No," Bailey said. "There has to be another explanation."

"It doesn't matter." I swallowed hard. "It's too late anyway."

"It's never too late to do the right thing, Nine," Bailey said, and I hated that she was right.

"You're going to run into him sooner or later." Paige dropped her hand.

"Why?" My gaze darted between them both.

"Because he got back last night," Paige answered.

Oh, fucking hell.

Okay, so he hadn't decided to stay in Canada like I secretly hoped and dreaded. Perfect.

I blew out a breath, glancing down at my belly. "It doesn't change anything," I said. "I highly doubt he spent the last six months thinking about our one-night-stand and saying *you know I'm done with my bachelor ways, I want to be a daddy.*"

I chuckled, and the girls did, too.

"You never know until you talk to him." Bailey hugged me from behind, and Paige hugged me from the front. Together we made one poorly shaped triangle of love, but it was exactly what I needed.

"And if he hasn't changed? If he's mad at me for keeping the baby?" I whispered, terrified to speak my worst fears too loudly.

"He would never say that," Paige said, releasing me.

"He's a good man. A beast but a good one." Bailey said, stepping back.

"What Shark isn't?" I asked, trying to joke but the nerves were quickly suffocating me.

I would have to see Warren.

I'd have to look him in those dark, sexy eyes, and show him what our night—and morning—of passion had created.

And I had to hope to God that seeing him wouldn't instantly turn me into some weeping damsel due to hormones and seeing the biological father of my child.

Because honestly, I could handle this on my own. I knew I could.

But if he wanted to be a part of it?

Be in my life, in the baby's?

I wasn't sure if I was strong enough to do both.

And that is what scared me most of all.

"All right," I finally said. "You tell me where they'll be next, and I'll talk to him."

Both of the girls smiled.

"They have a pick-up game tomorrow," Bailey said.

"Of course, they do," I said, rolling my eyes. I held my stomach. "Well, baby. I guess we couldn't hide forever."

CHAPTER 2

WARREN

GAGE HIT the puck with only half the ferocity he usually did, not wanting to risk hurting himself in a simple pick-up game. Still packed a hell of a punch. Gliding across the ice, I soared around him, blocking his attempt at the goal.

"Bailey and the kids keep you up all night?" I teased.

"Every night, man. Every. Night." He laughed, now merely skating than playing.

We'd already been at it for a few hours, and while the guys over in the Canadian camp had kept me in shape, it was nothing compared to playing against my boys. I was beat, but happy.

"I've missed you guys," I said and waved off their exaggerated *awws*. "Fuck you," I said as Rory skated over to us.

"No, it's cute," Rory said. "I mean, you did practically ghost us for six months."

I scoffed. "For the last time I didn't ghost anyone," I said. "My cell got wrecked the day I went over there, and I lost all my data. Everything. Wiped clean."

Rory skidded to a stop near the box, and Gage and I followed.

"Just think," Rory said, waving his hand in the air. "All those women's numbers, *gone*."

I cringed.

He wasn't wrong, but while I'd been over there only *one* woman had been on my mind.

Almost annoyingly so.

A pretty prefect blonde chef—my one wild night with Jeannine had ruined me for any Canadian beauties that sauntered my way. I hadn't been with anyone since like Jeannine had put some kind of voodoo on my dick.

Now that I was back?

I wanted her.

Again and again.

That in of itself was shocking and terrifying and had kept me from asking Rory or Gage to give me her number.

"Whoa," Rory said, dropping his arm. "You aren't sad about that at all, are you?" His helmet off, he narrowed his eyes at me, Gage mirroring a look of *what the fuck?*

"Did you meet someone over there?" Gage asked, sweat rolling down his face. From how hard we hit the ice, we were all drenched. I wiped some away with the back of my arm.

"Nah, man. Of course, not."

How could I when I couldn't get Jeannine's flavor off my tongue?

The sound of my name on her lips when she moaned.

The way she pushed back with every ounce of fire inside her, never giving an inch.

"Then why aren't you pining over the loss of all your contacts?" Rory asked.

Good question. One I didn't have time or energy to puzzle out.

"Because," I said. "It was months ago. I'm over it." I

shook my head. "And besides," I continued. "I legit texted you two my new number like the second day out there. We talked."

They laughed at that.

"We talked maybe a handful of times," Gage said.

"And?"

"And it was only when *we* called you," Rory added.

I punched Gage in the chest. "Aww, were you guys hurt I didn't check in every night before bedtime? Don't you have your wives for that kind of cuddly-crap?"

Rory and Gage shared a look before rolling their eyes.

"Anyway," I said, ready to get off the topic. "I'm back now. What did I miss?"

"Not much," Gage said. "Lettie is slaying kindergarten." I noted the hint of fear creep across his eyes before he blinked it away. "The rookie stepped up all season. Reaching out. Came to a couple of poker games."

"No shit?" I glanced to Rory for confirmation. He nodded. "Whoa," I said. "You trying to replace me with a younger model?"

"No, dear," Gage said. "Bentley is trying. So am I. We both know I won't be a Shark forever." He rolled his shoulder almost subconsciously. "I feel good knowing I've at least groomed the kid constantly vying for my spot."

I nodded, my respect for Gage never ceasing to deepen. The man had been through hell and back—the battle with his ex-wife, the securing custody of his daughter, an injury that almost took him off the ice for good, falling for his best friend, a new baby boy he'd never thought he was capable of having—all of it could've broken a lesser man. And now Gage was helping the rookie instead of fighting him.

"I still knock his ass around on the ice," Rory said.

I laughed. "Naturally."

"But now it doesn't end in smartass remarks. Well, not always," Gage said. "Mostly it's all about bettering himself. His technique. Wait till you see him."

"Oh, I'm holding my breath."

Gage punched me on the shoulder for the sarcastic remark.

"Anything else I missed? How are the girls?"

Gage tilted his head. "I already told you—"

Rory laughed, a shit-eating grin on his face. "He means Bailey, Paige, *and* Jeannine, not Bailey and Lettie."

I swallowed hard, glaring at Rory.

"What?" He shrugged. "Tell me I'm wrong."

I kept my lips sealed.

"Oh, come on, man," he continued. "I saw you two before you left. At the bar? It looked like you were about to—"

"You know I never kiss and tell," I cut him off.

And I didn't. Not even with the guys. Sometimes, they saw a woman leaving my apartment, and there was no denying it. But they hadn't seen Jeannine, and I hadn't told them a thing about that night.

Maybe because it had *lingered.*

Left a sweet craving in my mouth.

Maybe it was because she was friends with their wives and I felt like I'd crossed some sort of line.

Maybe it was all bull shit.

"Paige is fantastic," Rory said, a faraway look in his eyes. "Motherhood has turned her into a damn goddess. And Daphne..." He chuckled. "She's got me wrapped around her tiny little finger."

"That's awesome, man," I said, smacking his chest hard enough to make him wince. "Can't believe I get to be an uncle three times over." Lettie, Ethan, and Daphne were three slices of perfection—made more so that I could love them and then give them back to their parents at the end of the night. All fun, no work.

"Right?" Gage asked, tilting his head at me. "Wait till you see how big Ethan and Daphne have gotten. You're going to want one of your own."

A sharp laugh. "I'm not dad material," I said. "You both know that."

"You think either of us were before we got the call?" Rory looked between Gage and me.

"True," Gage said. "You don't know until you know."

"Well, I *know*," I said. "Hockey is my life. And when that's over..."

I knew I only had a few prime years left—sure, I could push it well into my forties, but those guys usually ended up with all kinds of injuries.

No, I wanted to retire in style. But until then, I'd be the best at the one thing I'd ever been good at—hockey. And after that...then who knows? Maybe I would want to be a dad like my friends. Maybe not.

So many maybes today.

"How is Jeannine?" I couldn't help but ask. I'd bounced around the question, and neither of them had taken the bait.

"She's good," Gage said, glancing at Rory.

"We think," Rory added.

Something twisted my gut. "What do you mean, you think?"

Rory shrugged. "She's been wrapped up in her restaurant," he said. "Has some kind of huge investment banquet in a couple months. Trying to get the funds and go-ahead for another location."

"We haven't seen her," Gage said. "Bailey and Paige always go to her place when their schedules come together."

"But hopefully that'll die down after this banquet stuff is over," Rory said. "I miss her cooking." He jolted, his eyes darting around the empty rink. "Don't tell Paige I said that."

We laughed and then something hot and pulsing snaked through my blood.

If Jeannine was stressed over this investment business, who better to offer her a little release? The idea simmered in my blood, begging me to head to *Nine's*—her flagship restaurant—right now and see if she was game.

Fuck, just the flash of her riding me had me growing hard right here in my gear.

What the hell?

I hadn't gotten hard for any bunny who hopped my way at the Olympics—hell, I hadn't even touched one—and one *thought* of Jeannine needing me, needing that sweet relief, had me raging while talking to my boys.

The woman had *definitely* placed voodoo on my dick.

"Speak of the red-headed devil," Rory said, sliding across the ice like a magnet pulled him. A flash of red hair, then brown.

Gage skated over as quickly as Rory had.

Bailey held their fourteen-month-old son on her hip, planting a quick but thorough kiss on Gage's lips.

Paige had Daphne in some sort of cloth wrap contraption, the little redhead sleeping soundly against her mom's chest, despite the kiss Rory planted on her.

I dropped the puck on the ice, shuffling it with my stick, keeping my eyes focused on the black against the white in an attempt to not be a third-wheel to the uber-love fest. They were blocking the exit to the locker rooms, and while I totally wanted to hold both babies, I wasn't about to brave smacking lips and love-struck sharks to do it.

"Warren," Jeannine's voice struck a hot chord through the center of my body, and I snapped my eyes up.

The woman was like a lightning strike—sharp, stunning and dangerously beautiful. Her long blond hair was gathered in a messy knot on her head, her face fresh, her kissable lips pink and perfect. I skated over to her with a sly grin on my face.

It had been six months.

Six months of obsessing about her laugh, the way she took a shot, the way she dug her nails into my back. I could practically taste her kiss, feel her silk folds against my tongue.

Lock it up.

I'd never reacted this way to a woman before. Especially not one I had a one-night-stand with, but what could I say? Jeannine had done something to me.

Voodoo. Right.

The blades of my skates shredded ice as I skidded to a halt before her. I trailed my eyes up and down her body, and my heart fucking stopped.

My brain slowed down, moving at a snail's pace.

First, I saw her belly—round and beautiful under her tight black shirt, like she'd swallowed a basketball.

Second, something warm pulsed in my blood with how damn sexy she looked in those yoga pants and comfy boots. I'd never seen the woman without her six-inch heels.

Third, anger roared in my chest, and I gripped my stick so hard I was shocked it didn't snap.

No one had told me she was pregnant.

The guys hadn't mentioned she was totally off the market.

Damn it.

A weight in my chest dropped all the way to my stomach, and I glared at the guys.

Bailey and Paige were tugging them away, Gage and Rory both looking shocked.

I flashed them a look that promised I'd deal with them later.

"Jeannine," I said, finally, trying not to snap.

She didn't belong to me.

We'd never said we were anything more than one wild night, but fuck me if I hadn't wanted to repeat it.

"Warren," she said again, her chest rising with a deep breath.

Some primal instinct deep inside me twitched at the way her swollen breasts moved.

God, they were perfect before but now they seemed so much more supple, round, begging for a bite.

"You're back," she said.

"Congratulations are in order it seems," I said, motioning toward her gorgeous belly. "Who is the lucky man who tied down the wild Nine?"

I hated that I sounded bitter. We'd both agreed there were no strings between us. That was *always* the arrangement for anyone I took to bed, and the women knew it up front. And it was *six* months ago.

Still.

I couldn't resist the urge to seek the fucker out who stole my second shot with her and pummel him into the pavement.

A dark laugh tumbled from her lips, her eyes glittering with a sharp edge. "You're joking right?"

I raised my brows. "Excuse me?"

Did she not want me to congratulate her?

Would she rather I show her how irrationally angry I really am?

She shifted her weight, rolling her eyes toward the ceiling. "You're going to pretend like you don't know what this is about?"

My head snapped back like she'd hit me.

I narrowed my gaze, sliding as close as possible to the half-wall that separated us. I towered over her so much she had to arch her neck to meet my eyes. Hers were a molten blue, churning with heat and a hint of anger.

What the fuck?

"Rory and Gage didn't tell me," I said. "So, how was I supposed to know?" I shook my head. "And besides, why does it matter?"

She gaped at me.

"I left you a message."

I furrowed my brow. "My cell broke the first day over there. I lost everything." I sighed. "But you're a free woman, Jeannine," I continued. "You didn't need to call and ask my permission to sleep with other people."

I would've told her not to.

That realization was even more evident now that I'd set eyes on her again.

Heard that fire in her voice.

Seen the spark in her eyes.

This woman...fuck, I would've loved to explore more with her.

Now it is too late.

Her eyes darted over every inch of my face like she was looking for a sign.

After a few seconds, another dark laugh flew from her lips, and she swiped under her eyes.

"Perfect," she said. "Fucking perfect," she muttered under her breath.

Something colder than the ice I stood on snaked into my veins.

Her tone was too devastated, too scared.

"Are you in trouble, Jeannine?" I almost growled.

What if the father of her baby was a shit guy pulling an up and run?

"Because if you need help, I'm here." My fingers flexed on the stick. "I'll do whatever you need, just tell me."

Holy shit that's true.

She could ask me to maul the guy right now, and I wouldn't hesitate.

Who am I?

Acting a shit ton like Gage and Rory, that's who.

I had *no* claim to this woman and yet everything inside me was dying to help her, soothe her, fuck her.

What the hell is wrong with you? She's pregnant!

She was my friend before—I'm allowed to react this way over a friend in need.

Even if all my hopes were killed at another shot with her.

Something softened in her eyes, and her shoulders dropped.

"I'm six months pregnant, Warren."

"So," I said too fast. "It's never too late to ask for help. And if you're in trouble, I want to be the one who—" My throat closed, choking off my words. Heart racing, I looked from her belly to her eyes and back again.

"Six months?" I coughed out.

She popped a hand on her hip and nodded.

"You're not saying..."

It couldn't be.

Fuck, we skipped the condom.

"Birth control," I whispered, unable to form a sentence.

She snorted. "Yeah, that tiny percent chance?" she shook her head. "Someone up there was desperate for there to be another Shark in the world."

My eyes widened as warmth slicked over my skin.

Mine.

I gazed at the curve of her stomach.

Mine.

The blue of her eyes.

Mine.

Without warning, the warmth shifted to flames, and I slammed my stick on the ice.

"Six months!" I snapped. "You've known for *six months* and didn't think I'd want to know?"

"I left you a message," she fired back.

"A message? Are you fucking kidding me, Nine?"

"I..." she sighed. "I thought you didn't care."

"What?"

"We knew what we were doing," she said. "Neither of us want...wanted this." She rubbed her hand over her stomach, and my knees about damn near buckled.

"You should've tried harder."

"And what were you going to do, Warren?" She glared at me. "Huh? Skip the Olympics?"

"Yes!" I shucked my gloves and raked my fingers through my sweat drenched hair. "I missed an entire season, but I would've *rushed* home right after the games! I would've taken care of you!"

"I don't need anyone to take care of me!"

The truth in her words hit me like a fucking shot to the

gut. So much so I skated back a few feet like the woman could slay me where I stood with just a single look.

This is a courtesy.

She doesn't want me to be in her life.

Our baby's life.

Acid raged hard and sharp, stinging every cell in my body.

"Then why the hell are you here?" The words were out of my mouth before I could stop them.

She gasped, her perfect pink lips popping into an O shape. She wetted them before setting me with another glare. "You deserved to know." She shook her head, turned on her boots, and walked away.

The sight of it carved something out of my chest, leaving me cold.

"I deserved to know *months* ago!" I shouted, unable to control the adrenaline racing through my veins as she exited the rink.

Mine.

I don't remember how I wound up in the locker room.

Or how I managed to crack the wood boards of my locker until I felt the skin on my knuckles split.

Rory and Gage were showered and dressed, waiting for me with guilt covered faces.

I bounded over to them, but neither flinched. Both stood their ground, prepared to help siphon off the anger if I needed it.

That alone was enough to make me see clearer.

"How could you two *not* tell me?"

"We didn't know," Gage said, looking at Rory then back at me. "We haven't seen her."

"She's never at the restaurant when we eat there," Rory

said. "Now that Paige told me, I realize she did it on purpose."

"Bailey, too," Gage said. "She always went over to Nine's place, never her over at ours."

"They didn't want us to know because Jeannine wanted to keep it her business."

I sank onto the bench, my head hanging between my shoulders.

Father.

I'm going to be a father.

"She doesn't want me in her life," I said, and I hated how damn defeated I sounded.

"What?" Gage snapped.

I shrugged.

"Did she say that?" Rory asked, surprisingly the calmest one in this room for once.

"She didn't try harder." I fisted my fingers. "She left one message. One. Does that sound like a person who wants help raising a child you created together?"

Fuck. We made a baby.

"Did she *say* she didn't want you in her life?" Gage asked.

"She said she didn't need anyone to take care of her."

Gage huffed and dropped down next to me. "Well, of course, she doesn't," he said, almost laughing but too smart to pull that shit right now. "She's *Jeannine.* The wildest one in our group of fiery girls. She'd never admit to needing help. That's why she kept it from us, too." The hint of anger in his voice made sense when I glanced at him.

She *had* kept it from them.

Even when they were all practically family after they married her best friends.

"Look," Rory said. "I don't know why she didn't try to

call every day. Or why she didn't at least tell us—"

"She knew we'd tell him," Gage interrupted.

Rory nodded. They were *my* best friends. They'd never leave me in the dark about something so huge, regardless of her asking them to keep it secret. I had a right to know. I *should've* known.

"But," Rory continued. "It probably doesn't help that she *knows* you."

"Thanks, I feel loads better." I rolled my eyes.

"No, man, hear me out." He sighed. "You've never been shy about telling people who your first love is."

My career.

My team.

"And," he said. "You and Jeannine were around each other enough to know neither of you had babies on the brain. Hell, I'm pretty sure she told *me* she never wanted kids."

"Right," Gage said. "She always reminded me of you when she talked like that." Gage flashed me a pitying look, and I glared at him. He shrugged.

"So," Rory went on. "That would be enough to not want to tell you. Or, she likely thought you got the message and didn't care."

I snarled. "I'm not a heartless asshole."

"I know," Rory said, holding up his hands. "I know, trust me. But she may not. Or she may have made herself believe this was some kind of burden to you."

Fuck.

"It's not," I said, shocked as hell those words came out of my mouth.

Because what had I always said?

What had I always thought?

That a wife and kids would be a distraction from the

game. From the career I spent my whole life working toward. One I was riding in my prime right now. One I didn't want to end any time soon. One I didn't want to choose between when it came down to it or something else.

But this? I hadn't prepared for this on any sort of level.

"What are you going to do?" Gage asked.

"I don't know," I said. "She was so pissed when she stormed out of here."

Rightly so.

"I was kind of a dick," I admitted.

"You were angry," Rory said. "That's totally understandable. We'd all be roaring if they'd hid it from us."

Gage nodded in agreement.

"What are you going to do?" he asked again.

"Talk to her?" I tilted my head. "If she'll let me." I unlaced my skates and bolted off the bench, needing a shower. A minute to get my head right. "I never wanted to be a dad," I admitted as I grabbed a towel from my bag. "But now..."

Now what?

I couldn't get Jeannine out of my head *before*.

Couldn't stop wondering what she was doing but was too much of a coward to call her.

I should've checked in.

I should've done a lot of things.

"Something shifted when she said the words," I said. "If she'll let me...I want to be there for her."

"How?" Rory asked.

A fair question.

One I wasn't close to having an answer too.

"I'll let you know when I figure it out."

Gage nodded, slinging his bag over his shoulder.

Rory did the same.

"We're here for you," Gage said. "Whatever you need."

"Thanks," I said, nodding as they headed out.

I walked in a fog to the showers, not really feeling the steaming hot water. Going through the motions, I wasn't really *there*.

I was with *her*.

Trying to change my reaction.

Trying to find a way to make her see I wasn't some guy who would check out when the stakes were raised.

She'll never believe you.

But that wouldn't stop me from trying.

CHAPTER 3

JEANNINE

"DAMN IT!" I snapped, slamming the copper skillet down and booking it out of the kitchen in my restaurant. I nearly knocked over Rafael on my way out.

My stomach rolled, and I barely made it to the bathroom. I heaved but had nothing left to give. I'd already thrown up everything at home before I came into work.

After a few minutes, and a few splashes of cold water to my face, I took a deep breath. "Baby," I said, holding my stomach. "Mommy needs you to cool it with this attitude. I know we had a shit day yesterday but please don't take it out on me."

Or do.

Since it's my fault.

Oh God, everything that happens to this child from now until I die will be *my* fault.

I leaned over the sink, another wave of nausea crashing over me for an entirely different reason.

"Jeannine?" Warren's voice sounded from the door, and my eyes snapped to it. One perfectly sculpted arm held open the ladies' room door, but his face was turned away.

"What are you doing here?" I asked, standing straight to inspect myself in the mirror.

My chef's coat was a bit tight due to the baby-ball-belly, but we didn't look half bad.

Not that I cared what Warren thought. His gruff response to me showing up yesterday was enough to shoot that fantasy all to shit.

"We need to talk," he said, still looking away.

I dried my hands, threw the crumpled paper towel in the trash, and brushed past him in a hurry. I stomped back into my kitchen, finding my copper skillet full of seared halibut had already been sent.

"Thanks, Rafael." The kid was brilliant and had been picking up my slack for the last couple of months. The second I was given the go-ahead by investors to open my fourth location, I was going to make him head chef. He still didn't have a clue.

"Jeannine," Warren said my name again, this time walking straight through my kitchen doors like he owned the place.

He didn't.

I did.

I glanced at the pile of tickets in the window, calling off orders as I read them.

"I'm not leaving until you talk to me," he said, crossing his arms over his chest.

Hot damn, that *chest*.

It was more defined than six months ago if that was possible. I hadn't been able to notice in all that hockey gear yesterday, but training with his native Canadians had turned the already sculpted man into a freaking Adonis. And the way his dark eyes stared me down, unwavering, unflinching...it was enough to make my body hum like a backup generator had started.

No, bitch. No!

I was horny as hell thanks to these hormones and not having an orgasm *since* the night of my little baby-ball's conception. But that didn't mean I was going to go all moony-eyed over Warren.

Not after yesterday.

"I assumed we talked everything out yesterday," I said, slipping a piece of salmon into a fresh skillet. The sizzle was a gorgeous sound I lived for.

The smell?

Fuck. My. Life.

I spun away as the steam rising from the pan hit my face, one hand on my back, the other on my tummy as I bent over the prep table next to my stove.

Deep breaths—in and out—I would not throw up every single time I cooked.

A pair of strong, warm hands were on my back, and without meaning to, I closed my eyes. My skin remembered his touch as it tightened with *need*.

"Are you all right?" he asked, his voice calm, steady.

Baby-ball wiggled as my heart rate soared, and suddenly the nausea was replaced with...*anger*.

I whirled around, jerking away from his touch. "No!"

I handed Rafael my tongs, silently telling him I'd be right back. He nodded, and I once again found myself loving that kid. I hurried out of the kitchen, turning left down the hallway, and flying into my office that was tucked into a back corner. Warren shut the door behind me, and I spun to face him.

"I'm *so* far from all right, Warren," I said his name like an insult.

This wasn't his fault.

Not really.

But he'd *hurt* me yesterday.

I never let men hurt me.

Never let them get close enough to sting.

Plus, I was *beyond* hormonal.

I flung my hand in the direction of the kitchen. "Lately, I can't smell any cooked protein without wanting to puke," I snapped. "Which is brilliant since I'm a fucking *chef*!" My breathing was ragged, but I pushed on. "The owner of the ancient building I've had my eye on for years is *finally* ready to sell to me. Because I know a few Sharks and he's a huge fan..." I eyed him, but the words kept coming. "I have this huge benefit in a few months to get the fourth location greenlit from investors, and the building owner, and the high-profile guest list isn't coming together like I planned."

I moved my fingers, pinching my thumb and forefinger together.

"And," I continued. "I just found out this morning that because my complex's yearly inspection turned up one *tiny* spec of black mold, the entire place has to be renovated. So, not only am I hugely pregnant, hormonal, and can't cook, but I've got no *home*." I huffed. "I'm supposed to *nest* soon! And I can't!"

I dropped my hand, smacking it against my black legging covered thigh. I had a pair in a variety of colors—the soft things had been a godsend since the first trimester.

Warren's arms were loose at his sides, his eyes sincere, tuned-in.

Relief washed over me so much I was slightly dizzy.

I chuckled.

He cocked an eyebrow at me.

"What's funny?" He asked, and the words shot me straight back to *that* night.

The night that changed my life—sure, I was a chaotic mess right now, but it was worth it. I knew that in the creases of my soul—this baby was my world.

"It's not you," I said through my laughter. I instinctively smoothed my hand over my tummy. "I guess that is why people do this when they're married."

He tilted his head.

"So they have someone they can yell at without worrying about them leaving," I said, sucking in a sharp breath. "That felt fucking great."

Warren chuckled. "Glad to help."

The severity of his words stole the smile from my lips.

"Why are you here?"

His Adam's apple bobbed as his eyes fell to where I rubbed my tummy. Something flickered in those dark eyes, something that wasn't anywhere near the cocky sparks I was used to.

"I was an asshole." He drew his gaze back to mine. "Yesterday. Six months ago. Maybe my entire life."

I rolled my eyes. "Oh, stop it," I said, and shifted my weight. My left hip was hurting something fierce. "Yesterday, sure. Six months ago was fun and you know it. And before that? You never lied about who you were to anyone. That doesn't make you an asshole."

"Debatable," he said, the gruffness to his voice eliciting warm chills all over my body.

Great.

"Look," he said. "I want to be here for you. For the baby." His voice cracked on the last word, and it was enough to sting my heart.

"I didn't tell you because I needed anything from you. I

know you never wanted kids. I'm not a bunny trying to trap you into anything."

"Fuck, woman." He snorted. "I *know* you don't need me."

Good.

"I'm saying *I* need you."

My eyes widened, and he quickly raised his hands like he was trying to tame a wild animal.

"Don't freak out," he said. "I'm not about to pull a diamond. I just...I want a chance, Jeannine. Give me a chance to prove to you I'd be a good dad and a good...well, other things if that time comes."

It was my turn to tilt my head. "I can't."

He sighed. "You have to."

"Warren," I said, the word getting tangled in my throat. "This was never part of either of our plans. We were the same. Career-focused, loved the single life. That was us, and I was fine with that. The second I saw those two pink lines? Everything changed for me. It doesn't have to for you, but I can't let this baby get hurt. In any way."

"Fuck," he said, shaking his head. "I should've been here. Stupid Olympics. Fucking dumbass phone."

I pressed my lips together to hide my smile. I'd never seen the beast of a Shark flustered. It was kind of endearing.

Kind of sexy AF too.

I hushed the inner purring kitten that only woke up in Warren's presence.

"Please, Nine. The last thing I want to do is hurt the baby, or you. I know you have no reason to trust me, but I want to be part of your life."

I rubbed my palms over my face, every protective instinct battling inside me.

"Let me prove it to you," he said before I could come to a decision.

"What do you mean?"

He took two steps closer to me, the heat from his body filling my space. I arched my neck to meet his eyes because he was so damned tall.

I could climb him in two seconds. Even with the baby-ball he wouldn't struggle...

Down girl.

"Give me these last three months. Let me show you the kind of man I want to be. For you. For the baby."

"I don't know—"

"Do I have to beg?" He raked his fingers through his hair. "I'll pay—"

"I don't need your money," I snapped.

"I know," he said. "I know." His dark eyes lit up. "This benefit, the owner...he's a fan? I'll be there. I'll take photos and sign anything he wants."

Hope bloomed dangerously in my chest. I did need a Shark, but I figured I'd rope Gage or Rory into it. Having Warren there...

"There has to be something you need," he continued, taking my silence as a no. "Maybe help with a *list*?"

My blood froze in my veins.

Damn these Shark boys gossip like old ladies!

"What are you talking about?" I tried to play dumb.

He smirked, reading the lie all over my face. "Gage and Rory mentioned you girls all made lists. They didn't go into full details, but if Bailey and Paige have a list, you do too. Give me three months, and I'll help you check off everything on that list. If by the end of the three months you don't want me in your and the baby's life, I'll go quietly."

I laughed again. "You have no idea what you're suggesting."

"Yes, I do," he said, the hint of lust flashing in his eyes.

Flashes of him on his knees before me, hovering on top of me, rocking inside me—it made me tremble. How could he possibly think about having sex with me when I was basically a whale?

"No," I said. "You don't."

"Enlighten me," he challenged.

"Bailey and Paige's lists may have been dirty-girl themed, but I *am* the dirty-girl who helped write them."

"That's okay."

"And *they* helped me write mine." More like Bailey grabbed the paper and Paige wrote items down, and I watched from behind a pitcher of margaritas. "They put things on the list that I have *never* experienced. Things I likely never would unless I went out on a limb and changed my lifestyle for a bit."

"I'm not following," Warren said, his eyes solely focused on me.

"It's a clean list. Couple stuff. Chick-flick-nights, farmer's markets, brunch." I had to give the man credit—he didn't flinch. If anything, he looked *excited*.

"Oh, I'm all over that," he said.

"What?" I gaped at him. "You can't be serious! That list doesn't sound anything like *us*."

He smirked. "And I'm sure Paige and Bailey's lists were nothing like them." He cocked a knowing eyebrow at me. "Give me this three months, Jeannine. And that list."

I hesitated. I couldn't afford to fall for this man. Not when I knew his lifestyle—hell, I'd *been* him six months ago.

But, I could allow him to be in the baby's life...*if* he

proved he was in this for real.

"You can't fall in love with me," I said, mimicking the words we'd spoken to each other six months ago.

He pushed some hair off my face, the damn touch igniting a trail of fire over my skin.

Damn, it's been too long again.

"Same goes for you," he said.

"No worries here." I smiled, hoping the confident mask would hide the icy-fear shooting through my veins.

Seven months ago this proposition might've been an entertaining fling. Something I tried to complete my list and have a little fun at the same time. But it wasn't just about me anymore. It never would be again. And while I was completely fine with that fact, I didn't think Warren had a clue what was in store for him.

Warren leaned closer to my face, his nose just a breath away from mine. "So, we have a deal?"

I nodded, unable to speak. He smelled so good, crisp and spicy and alluring. The heat from his body snaked around mine like a tempting string of pleasure begging to be plucked, and my body remembered how well he could play me.

"Perfect," he said, drawing back as I'd gone lusty-eyed under his spell. He backed toward the door, his hand on the knob. "Oh, and Jeannine?" He asked after opening it.

"Yeah?"

"I need your keys."

I scrunched my forehead at the hand he held palm up as if I'd toss him my keys without question.

"The guys and I aren't working," he said. "Off-season."

"So? Why does that matter? And what does it have to do with my keys?"

"We'll move your stuff into my place while you finish

your workday," he said, that cocky grin on his lips.

"Excuse me?"

He sighed, almost like he finally realized the massive challenge I was.

Good, better to learn that sooner.

"Nine. You said you have black mold in your apartment—"

"A tiny spec—"

"I don't care. I wouldn't let you or the baby near it even if they weren't renovating." The protective growl in his voice made a shiver ripple inside my core, and my knees weakened.

Stay strong. Stay strong.

"Please," he said, those eyes going all soft and open and vulnerable. Fucking hell. "I have more room than I could ever need. You can take the master, and I'll sleep in one of the guest rooms. Hell, I'll sleep in the guest house if you want me to." He finally dropped his hand when he realized I hadn't budged to get my keys. "I'll sleep at Rory's?"

I chuckled, shaking my head as I grabbed my purse and fished out my keys. The man was committed, I'd give him that. And if his house was anything like Gage's, then there would be tons of room. It would be nice not having to stay a hotel for the next three months, or at one of the girl's—they didn't need my preggo attitude on a constant basis, not with their own babies to take care of.

I moved slowly, stopping an inch away from him. "I suppose if we're going to pretend to be a couple to complete that list, moving in together will only make things easier." I closed the keys into his hand.

"Thank you," he whispered, almost like he didn't mean to say it out loud.

I chuckled again. "You do realize you just agreed to

have a highly-hormonal, highly-pregnant woman move into your house? I mean, you *know* how tough I was to handle before you knocked me up."

"Oh, don't worry." He grinned, trailing a finger over the line of my jaw. "I can handle you."

Another shiver raked my skin as he winked and turned out the door.

I watched him walk away, the muscles in his back so gorgeously evident from the tight black shirt he wore.

I can handle you.

Well, I'm glad one of us was confident because living with Warren?

The sexy-as-sin, best lay of my life, father of my unborn child?

That was going to be some kind of newly invented torture, and I wasn't sure if I'd be strong enough to resist the temptation.

CHAPTER 4

WARREN

"HOW MANY PAIRS of shoes do you own?" I asked as I hefted the sixth and final clear plastic tub from her SUV.

All of them filled with shoes—kitten heels and fuck-me heels and boots. Each pair pristine and organized in their own box. A mental image of her wearing any of them—and *only* them—while I feasted on her from my knees, flashed red hot in my mind.

Fuck. Lock it up.

Rory and Gage had helped move her stuff into my house earlier today without hesitation. Each of them had their fair share of advice for living with a pregnant woman, but it was hard to know how much of it I should follow. Jeannine and I weren't like Bailey and Gage or Rory and Paige.

Nine hadn't fallen madly in love with me and *then* decided to have my child.

No.

I was lucky she was allowing me to give her a place to stay while her apartment was renovated. She was successful and resourceful—she could've shot down my offer and stayed with one of the girls or sublet another apartment until hers was fixed.

That notion alone gave me hope.

"Are you complaining?" She asked, falling into step behind me as I sat the tub down on my already crammed dining room table.

Most of her things—furniture, books, electronics—were now neatly stored in the guest house's master bedroom. The one I'd never furnished because I *never* had overnight guests. But there were some things she'd demanded stay with her. The killer cookware, for sure, her clothes, and the many bins filled with shoes.

"Of course, not," I said, resting an elbow on the lid of the box. "But are you sure you don't want these to go into storage with the rest of your stuff? The guest house isn't that far—"

She cut a glare that silenced my words.

"Point taken." I raised my hands in defense. "It'll take me a beat to clear the suits out of my master closet, but I'll get it done." I turned, heading to do just that.

"No," she said, and I spun back around. "You don't need to clear out your closet," she said, running her hand over the clear tubs. "I'll take the guest room. Besides, I can't exactly wear half of these." She sighed. "I mean I *could,* but I wouldn't dare risk falling off my heels and hurting the baby."

A warmth pulsed in my chest and I dared a glance down at her tummy. Something I'd avoided since she'd arrived twenty minutes ago.

Every beat of my heart screamed *mine, mine, mine.*

I wanted to run my hands over her belly and talk to the baby I never knew I wanted.

Wanted to *feel* what she felt—our lives coming together inside her to create something short of a miracle.

Damn.

I'd never thought anything would have the power to change me so drastically and so quickly, but here I was, moving Jeannine into my house. A place I'd never even brought a woman before—except Lettie and the girls—let alone allowed one to sleep over.

If I was being honest, those six months I spent thinking about Jeannine, most of those fantasies included sleeping with her *here*.

In my room, in my kitchen, on the damn dining room table now covered in all things *her*.

And that was before I knew about the baby.

"I just want them close," she said. "So I can take them out and look at them and remember the life I used to have." She gasped, her eyes flaring wide as her words caught up with her. "I didn't mean it like that," she hurried to continue. "I'm happy." She rubbed her belly, almost like she was apologizing to the baby. "I'm so beyond happy—"

"Hey," I said, stepping toward her with my hands outstretched like I was approaching a cornered animal. "It's okay to miss your old life." I stopped with a few inches between us. "It's only been six months," I said. "This will likely take more than a lifetime to get used to."

A small laugh and she nodded.

"I know you're right," she said. "I never want to sound like I have regrets. Because I don't." She locked her gaze on mine, the severity in those blue eyes shaking me. A few blinks and it softened. "We can put these in one of your guest room closet if that's all right."

"You're carrying my child," I said, no room for argument in my tone. "You're sleeping in *my* bed. No guest room."

A tiny sigh escaped her lips, and she darted her tongue out to wet them.

Heat shot straight to my dick with that innocent little move, and it took every ounce of willpower I possessed not to reach out and bury my hands in her silky hair.

To claim her mouth.

Taste her in more ways than a kiss.

"It has better back support," I said, my voice a damn near whisper.

"Okay," she said. "But we can still put the shoes somewhere else. As long as it's a closet and not some darkened storage unit."

I laughed. "You feel like a master bedroom in the guesthouse is a storage unit?"

"Well, it is now, isn't it?" She popped her hands on her hips.

I tilted my head and scooped up the same box I'd just sat down. "Guess you have a point," I said, heading to the guest room across from mine. "This space is free." The closet didn't have a thing in it save for some extra bedding my mom had bought as a house-warming gift after I'd purchased the place.

"Perfect," Jeannine said, peeking around the corner as I opened the door and sat the first tub down on the empty closet floor.

"One down," I said, laughing. "Four million to go."

She snorted. "If I made the kind of money a Shark does that number would be a hell of a lot more accurate."

I gaped at her, noticing she wasn't close to joking.

"What?" she stopped near where I'd halted in the doorway. "I have a weakness for shoes."

I shifted to face her like it wasn't an option *not* to—my

body begging to be aligned with hers in any way possible. "I didn't figure the wild Nine had any weaknesses."

She arched a brow at me. "A few."

"What are the others?" I leaned one arm on the doorframe, slightly caging her in.

"I'll never tell," she said, her chest rising and falling a bit faster than moments before.

I dared to shift closer, so close I could feel the heat from her body, smell the fresh scent of her skin.

"I could get it out of you." I kept my other hand steady at my side, demanding it not to betray me and reach for her.

"Is that so?"

I nodded, unable to stop the smile shaping my lips.

"And how would you go about getting that information from me?"

Yes. There she is. The girl who likes to play.

"Oh, I have a few techniques I think would work on you."

"Yeah?"

"Mmhmm." I inched my face closer to hers, needing more of her scent, more of her nearness. "Ways that would likely have you spill all your secrets."

A shudder rippled over her skin, and she forced out a laugh. "I don't have any secrets."

"Liar," I teased, my nose a breath away from the tip of hers.

"I'm an open book."

"I know that's not true."

"You don't know me," she countered, shifting so that her spine was against the doorframe, her body *almost* brushing mine.

I smirked. "You're independent and fierce and sometimes a real pain in the ass."

She rolled her eyes, but a flush raced over her cheeks.

"But," I continued, taking my time to trail my eyes over her body. "Under all that strength? There is something *there*. Something I think you rarely let people see. Maybe not even the girls."

Her lips parted, her eyes darting over mine.

They were shocked but hungry and full of heat.

She wanted something from me, and in that moment, I had something I wanted to give her.

One breath, that is all that separated my lips from hers. It would only take one nod from her, and I'd claim her mouth.

I held my breath, holding my position, waiting...wanting.

She tilted her chin up just a fraction and closed her eyes.

Submission.

Acceptance.

Mine.

A thrill rushed through me, flickering nerves fueling my racing heart as I smoothed my hand over her cheek.

She jolted, her eyes snapping open wide and panicked...

Before she sprinted from under my touch.

She *ran* away.

Leaving me standing there like a fucking idiot.

"Oh God," she moaned—but nothing like the way I remembered.

This was jagged and raw and...

Oh.

Oh.

I snapped out of the rejection and hurried to the bathroom down the hall.

Jeannine wretched through the closed door, and I cringed.

My hand on the knob, I paused before opening it.

"Can I come in?"

"Go. Away."

I pressed my lips into a line and took a deep breath.

"Let me help you," I tried again.

Another wave hit her, the sound stinging my stomach.

"Nothing can help me. Go, save yourself."

I bit my lip to hide the laugh.

This woman. Funny and smart and so damn stubborn.

A groan and a sigh and I *felt* the worst was over.

Still, I hurried to the kitchen, wetting a cloth with ice cold water.

Jeannine was coming out of the bathroom by the time I made it back. She eyed the rag, but I put my hand on the small of her back, guiding her into my bedroom. The touch was searing but innocent and definitely not nearly enough.

"Here," I said, gesturing for her to lay down. She obeyed, slipping under the covers easily enough.

The king size bed threatened to swallow her whole, and I focused on the light sheen of green on her skin to stop from noticing how incredible she looked in my bed. It didn't really stop me from picturing all the ways in which I wanted her.

"Rory told me this helps," I said, placing the rag on the back of her neck.

"It'll get your pillow all wet," she said, her voice so, so damn tired.

"I don't care," I said. "Better?" I asked when she'd closed her eyes against the cool contact.

She nodded.

"Good." I rubbed the back of my neck, not sure what to do. I wanted to sit down next to her and massage her back or front or feet or whatever she needed, but I knew she'd never tell me what she *actually* needed. I'd have to pay such close attention. "I thought morning sickness was supposed to ease by this point?" I asked, still standing there gazing down at her.

"So they keep telling me." She slowly opened her eyes. "What did you do last night, Google all things pregnancy related?" she joked.

I forced out a laugh, glancing at the floor.

"You didn't."

I shrugged. "Just a little." That was a lie. I'd spent hours reading up on everything—even some things I'd rather forget. "I may have had the guys give me a crash course, too."

She chuckled, but it was half-groan. "You didn't need to do that," she said, rolling to her left side, an arm draped protectively over her belly. "I've totally got this under..." she sucked in a sharp breath. "Control."

A blink and I was there, leaning over her, my arms supporting me as I neared her face.

"I get that, Nine," I said. "I really do. You don't need me. But I'm *here*."

Something flashed over her eyes—fear and hope and worry all mixed together.

I allowed myself one more innocent touch as I trailed a finger over her forehead, tucking the wild hairs away from her face. "Now, rest," I ordered. "I'm going to the store to stock up on crackers and ginger ale and anything else you want."

A small smile shaped her perfect, pouty lips. "You don't have to—"

My growl cut her off, and she glared at me.

"Ice cream," she said.

"What kind?"

"Chocolate." She sighed, her brow furrowing as something happened inside of her that I couldn't see. "Just chocolate."

"You got it," I said, shoving off the bed and fixing the covers over her. "You should sleep."

"It's nearly five pm."

"So?" I shrugged in the doorway. "You worked way too hard today." I cocked a brow at her, daring her to argue.

For once, she didn't. She simply closed her eyes and settled deeper against my pillows.

I tapped the doorway, turning.

"Thank you," I heard her say as I walked away.

"Anytime," I said back, not sure if she heard me, and not sure if she'd meant for me to hear her.

I grabbed my keys and sank behind the wheel of my car —my driver on standby during the offseason. Starting the ignition, I shook my head.

Jeannine had only been in my house for an hour, and we'd laughed, fought, and I'd been seconds away from kissing her.

It was going to be a long three months, especially if she continued to battle me at every turn.

A smirk shaped my lips as I backed out of my driveway.

Maybe it would be more fun than I could hope for.

CHAPTER 5

JEANNINE

"ARE YOU SURE, RAFAEL?" I asked, glancing around my kitchen like I'd never see it again.

"Yes, Chef," he said, even though I'd asked him for years to call me Jeannine or Nine.

"I don't want to put too much pressure on you," I said, but it was more like I didn't want to take these last three months off of work.

I did, but I didn't.

I'd *always* worked. And when I wasn't working, I *thought* about work. Even while I'd played up my single lifestyle, I did so with my career in mind.

"It's not," he said. "I promise. I can do this."

I knew he could. That's why he'd be my head chef over at the fourth location whenever I got the go-ahead to open it. This would be good practice for him, and I'd get some much-needed time away from throwing up constantly because of the food smell.

Yesterday flashed through my mind—the way Warren had been so gentle and yet so damn primal as he ordered me to rest and let him take care of me. I wasn't used to it, and every instinct roared at me to *not* get used to it...but it was nice.

Surprising.

And he *had* helped.

"The doctors assure me once I have the baby I'll be back to normal and able to handle all the smells again."

He nodded. "We'll be glad to have you back then, but in the meantime," he said. "Just go. Rest. Don't worry about this. Take care of that proper tiny chef." He pointed to my stomach. "And then you'll come back, likely with a new menu and as brilliant as ever."

I wrapped him in a hug. "You're seriously the best."

"I know," he teased. "Now go."

I took one last glance around, silently promising my first baby—my restaurant—I'd be back. "I'm only a phone call away if you need anything," I said as I walked toward the doors. "And I'll still be overseeing the benefit and preparing for it."

"You're the boss, boss. Always will be." He waved at me before glancing up to look at the incoming tickets. The boy was good. And I'd never be able to thank him enough for this time.

The grin was still on my face as I sank into Warren's SUV parked outside the restaurant. This time he was behind the wheel, looking delicious in a pair of dark jeans and white long-sleeved henley.

"Everything go okay?" He asked as I buckled my seatbelt.

"As good as it could."

"You going to be okay?"

"Yeah," I said. "I think. It's just crazy...the idea of not working for four or so months." Because while this three-months off was a luxury, the next two would be a necessity. For the baby.

Holy hell baby we're not too far off.

I was assaulted with three big kicks as if baby-ball heard me.

"I know," he said, pulling out of the parking lot and onto the street. "The first time we hit off-season, I wasn't sure what to do with myself. The guys and I made a habit of going to the gym every day, doing pick-up games, that kind of thing, but the stillness...it's enough to drive you crazy."

"Gee thanks," I said, rolling my eyes.

He chuckled. "Sorry. It's not like you're being still, though." His eyes flashed to my tummy for a brief second before returning to the road. "You're working even when you're not working."

"True." I rubbed my hands over my stomach. "So, where are we headed today?" I asked, ready to change the subject and get my mind off leaving work. It would take more than a few days to get used to.

"Crossing a number off the list," he said.

Butterflies joined the kicking baby in my tummy. Any number on that list would be completely new territory for me. Good thing I was being pretty flexible about embracing the *new*.

"And you're still certain this is what you want to spend your off-season doing?" I asked, glancing at him from the passenger seat.

He shifted his eyes to me for only a moment. "There is nowhere I'd rather be right now."

Heat flushed my cheeks, but I blamed the hot-flash on the bun in my oven. It had nothing to do with the sexy man with all the right words behind the wheel.

Off-season, remember? He wouldn't be doing any of this if he had games to play.

It wasn't fair, but I couldn't stop the thought.

I had to be careful.

Warren's help was temporary. We both knew it. His career was everything to him, and I couldn't blame him for it. That is how I used to be, too, before...everything changed.

Ten minutes later, he'd parked the SUV in a giant grassy parking lot.

"A carnival?" I asked as I got out of the car. My boots squished in the grass that was half-soaked in last night's rain. The Seattle sky was a beautiful slate-gray, but not a rain cloud in sight.

"Number six on the list. I was lucky. This is its last day before they pack up and move on." He reached for my hand, easily intertwining our fingers as he tugged me toward the entrance.

He paid for our entry and walked us onto the grounds. Several colorful rides, including a Ferris wheel, were scattered about, kids screaming and running back and forth.

"You know I can't ride any of these, right?" I asked as we walked through the crowds.

"Jeannine," he said, chiding. "I may be a Shark, but I'm not dumb."

I chuckled. "Just double checking."

"This is on the list," he said. "And there are more than just rides."

"Like?"

"There are food trucks," he said and motioned toward the left where a line of trucks sat. "And games." He glanced to the right where row after row of game booths lined the grounds, all complete with the gaudy and brightly colored stuffed animal prizes.

He stopped in the middle of the two paths. "Which do you want to do first?"

I smiled up at him, totally out of my element. I hadn't been on a real date since high school, and even then, I'd cut out early. Though, I supposed this wasn't exactly real was it? It was an item off a list and a way for Warren to prove his worth for the baby.

It wasn't for *me*.

"Food," I said.

"Yes!" He tugged us to the left. "I'm starved."

"*You* are?" I laughed as he stopped us in front of the first truck. "I could eat enough for two, maybe three."

He jolted, his eyes widening as they focused on my stomach. "Is it...are they...*twins*?"

I laughed at his panicked expression. "No," I finally said. "Not twins."

The breath that released from him made his tight shoulders loosen. "I mean," he said quickly. "That would've been fine. I just needed a minute to adjust."

I gazed up at him, trying to read his eyes. There was no bullshit there. Only true panic followed by true acceptance.

Maybe Warren was being real.

Maybe he wanted this.

I focused harder on the chalkboard menu.

"Fried oreos?"

"Have you had one before?" He asked like everyone was eating them.

"Yeah, no."

He gaped at me. "Buckle up."

I laughed as we moved up in the line. A few minutes later, he'd ordered us two. He handed me the deep-fried circle wrapped in parchment paper, and we stepped into the next line for the next truck.

"Cheers," he said, tapping his oreo against mine.

Timidly, I brought the dessert to my mouth and crunched. The combination of the chocolate cookie and crispy, slightly salty, outer shell was explosive.

"Oh," I moaned, devouring the rest of the cookie. "Holy hell."

"Right?" He finished his off, taking our empty papers and wadding them up in a ball. He tossed them in the trashcan that separated the lines for the different trucks.

"I've never thought of deep frying a cookie." I laughed.

"What about that crispy brownie thing on your menu?" He asked as we waited. "Isn't that deep fried?"

I snapped my gaze to him, shocked he knew one of the items off my menu. "You've had my filo-dough brownie before?"

"It's my favorite," he said, tilting his head. "Why are you looking at me like that?"

"It's mine too," I said, and blinked a couple of times, replacing my shock with a genuine smile. "I didn't realize you'd eaten at my place enough to find a favorite."

He shrugged. "You do remember that my boys are madly in love with your two best friends...right?"

I laughed. "How could I forget that?" I glanced down. "Bailey's celebrate-Warren-going-to-the-Olympics-party is when this happened." I held my tummy with both hands.

He gazed down at it, a sense of wonder glazing his eyes.

"Sorry," I said, and he blinked out of his daze.

Likely he'd traveled back to that party and put a condom on after I'd asked him not to.

The thought made a flare of grief shoot through me, and

I'd never been more certain that I was always meant to have this baby than I was in that moment.

"Why?" He asked as we moved up another space in line.

I shrugged. "I didn't know if...if it bothered you for me to bring up that night."

"It doesn't." He retook my hand, squeezing it. "I promise." He sighed. "I know it's going to take time for you to believe that, but that's what we're here for."

I smirked. "Here, at the carnival..."

He rolled his eyes. "You know what I mean."

I did.

That was something I'd never had trouble with before.

Reading Warren had always been easy back when we'd hang out at the numerous group functions when our friends got together. But now, I found myself floundering. Sometimes it was just as easy. Others it wasn't.

"So," he said, stepping up to the truck's window. "What will it be? Crab wonton sandwich with sriracha coleslaw, or the pulled pork sandwich with the sweet potato fries?"

I raised my eyebrows. "You try one. I'll try the other."

"Sounds perfect," he said and placed our orders.

Easy. Fun. No drama.

For two people not used to dates, we were doing pretty good so far.

One sandwich, a basket of fries, and half a funnel cake later, I had to throw in the towel. "Okay," I said. "Game time."

"What?" Warren teased. "The pregnant lady gives up first?"

I laughed, holding my stomach. "If baby-ball here decides to do somersaults, you aren't going to like what you see. I need to quit while we're ahead."

He chuckled. "Noted."

We walked to the other side of the carnival, dodging kids, pre-teens, and their parents as we made it to the line of game booths.

"You a good shot?" He asked, stopping at the first booth. It had a row of guns facing a wall of various sized targets.

"Not that I know of," I said.

"Let's see what you're made of." He paid the attendant, and I picked up the gun that was attached to the table with a chain. His muscles flexed under his shirt, and paired with the light laughter in his eyes, I had a hard time breathing.

Finally, I picked up my gun, the thing heavier than my cast iron skillet.

"Bring it," I said, finding my voice and aiming at the first target.

A whirring sound flew through the booth, and the freaking targets started moving.

"Oh, hell," I said, laughing as I pulled the trigger. I missed every single target.

Warren hit five, but you had to hit them all to win a prize.

"Maybe next time," I said as we sat the guns down and moved on to the next booth.

"How's the food settling?" He asked as we waited our turn at the dart booth.

"Good so far," I said, glancing down at my belly like it would tell me if it had other plans.

"Good," he said, stepping up to take our turn. This game had a wall of balloons. Pop four and win. With only five darts, the odds were slim.

"Damn," I said as all my darts stuck into the felt-covered wall behind the blown-up balloons. "I'm no good at these games."

Warren popped three but missed the other two. He chuckled as we moved on to the next one. "Winning isn't the point. It's just about having fun. They're all rigged anyway."

I arched a brow at him. "How is it one of the most competitive Sharks is totally chill about losing?"

"Maybe it's because I win when it matters."

A zing of electricity bolted down my spine with the sincere look in his dark eyes.

I tilted my head, stopping at the next booth. This was the one with the hammer and the bell at the top. You had to ring the bell to get a prize.

"So," I said, a smirk on my lips. "You're saying if I made this important to me...you'd win?"

"Yes," he said.

I glanced upward, my eyes on the array of colored prizes. It was like a stuffed animal rainbow. I pointed to a fluffy purple puppy. "I want that."

He cocked a brow at me. "Seriously?"

"Yes," I said, challenging him. "It would mean a lot to me. It's super cute and purple is my favorite color."

"Good to know," he said, strutting up the booth and handing the man his money.

"Good luck, dude," a stacked bearded guy said as he handed him the hammer. "I tried three times."

Warren raised his eyebrows, surmising the huge man. If he couldn't hit it...

Warren didn't even groan as he lifted the massive hammer over his shoulders. He stared up at the bell like it was an enemy, the competitive look flashing over his eyes that I only ever saw when he was on the ice.

In one fluid swing, he brought the hammer down on the center of the weight, the tiny metal ball flying upward only to stop a centimeter before the bell. It came crashing back down, the sound almost tragic.

The look of defeat in his eyes hit straight to my chest. Perhaps I shouldn't have picked this game to challenge him on. I knew better than anyone how strong he was. He didn't have to prove it.

"It's okay," I said, smiling. "Honestly, I was just kidding."

He shook his head and handed the attendant another five-dollar bill.

Another swing.

Another miss.

"Warren," I said. "I swear it's fine. It's rigged. You said it yourself."

He narrowed his gaze, looking from me, to my belly, to the purple puppy, and back again. He rubbed his palms together widening his stance as he took another swing.

No bell.

I crossed my arms over my chest, glancing around at the crowd that had now gathered around us—both kid and adult alike. Warren was as stubborn as me—if that was possible—because he handed the attendant another five.

Another swing. Another miss. Another five.

"Warren," I whispered, keeping my smile plastered for the crowd which now included a few people with their cell phones aimed at him.

"Come on, Kinley!" A kid in the crowd shouted. He wore a Sharks jersey with Warren's number on it. "You can do it!"

My heart melted as I watched that kid grin up at Warren. I'd forgotten what it was like to go out in public with a Shark.

Warren smiled at the kid, throwing him a thumbs up.

No pressure. I swallowed hard, now invested in this way beyond a silly challenge.

Warren rolled up the sleeves of his henley, his bulging forearms knotting something in my stomach. He put more distance in his stance and bent at the knees slightly. The determination on his face was enough to make my heart flip, but watching those muscles work as he hefted that hammer one more time, made my knees tremble.

He brought the hammer down, hard and straight to the weight's center. The bell shot up and up and up.

And it *rang.*

The crowd erupted into loud cheers and applause as if Warren had just shot a winning goal in a shootout.

I grinned like a school-girl, clapping, too.

The attendant gave him the purple puppy, and he handed it to me. The thing was wicked soft as I cradled it to my chest.

"See?" he asked. "I win when it matters."

I laughed. "You could've bought me ten purple puppies with how much money you spent to win this."

"That's not the point."

"Then what is?" I asked as the kid with Warren's jersey timidly walked up to him.

"The point is that you asked for something, and I gave it to you. Didn't matter how hard it was or how slim my odds were...I made it happen." He glanced from me to my tummy and back again before turning his attention to the kid.

"Mr. Kinley, will you please sign my jersey?" The kid asked, and Warren immediately fist-bumped him.

I watched as he signed his jersey, shook the kid's father's hand, and charmed the mother. I was awestruck, not because this beast of a man could be gentle, humble to his fans, but by his words.

He *was* taking this seriously. Even if he had to prove it in not-so-serious ways. Like winning an impossible purple puppy. I clutched the thing to my chest as we walked back to the car ten minutes later.

Words tangled in my throat the entire ride back to his house...my temporary home.

"Did you not have fun?" He finally broke the silence as he shut the front door.

"I did!" I answered a little too enthusiastically as we walked inside. "I really did, Warren." I looked down at the puppy still in my arms. "I'm kind of shocked."

"Ouch," he said, gripping the center of his chest.

"Stop," I said, giggling. "I meant about the date. I'm not used to dates."

He sighed, shoving his hands in his pockets. "Me either."

"You wouldn't know it," I said. "That was really wonderful."

"Yeah?" He asked, walking closer, stopping with only an inch between us.

He was right there.

Open. Ready. Willing.

Just like yesterday when he'd nailed me to my core—spouting that he *knew* me.

And from what he'd said?

He *did*.

The man had shown me the best time I'd had in so long, and here he was just waiting for me to take the reins. And I wanted to. So badly.

I wanted to let him in.

All the way in.

Let him take care of me, of the baby, all of it.

But that wasn't me.

And it wasn't him.

And we couldn't get caught up in this fantasy.

I cracked a smirk, hoping the confident mask hid the hunger in my eyes. I wanted this man like my next meal, but I couldn't let myself have him. Because I *knew* him, and the second the Shark's season started—we would be the last thing on his mind.

"I don't sleep with a man on the first date," I joked.

He chuckled, glancing down at my belly.

"I would never assume," he teased, but didn't back up an inch.

"Here," I said, handing him the puppy. "Sleep with this."

He took it, grinning. "I'll guard it with my life."

"You do that," I said, spinning around to head to my new room before I did something stupid like kiss him and beg him to fuck me. It had been so long, and he'd touched parts of me with that simple date that no man had ever touched before.

I wasn't thinking straight.

"See you in the morning," he called as I shut the door to my bedroom.

"See you!" I called back, my forehead against the door.

I locked it for good measure.

Not to keep him out, but to keep me from wandering the house in the middle of the night—a hormonal, lust-starved woman hunting for a Shark.

CHAPTER 6

WARREN

THE HOUSE SMELLED of fresh dough and sugar when I returned from my late morning run. An hour on the pavement had done wonders to work off the frustration coiling my muscles like a spring.

Until I walked into my kitchen.

Jeannine was in front of the stove, sliding pancake batter onto a griddle. It sizzled on the pan, the hiss barely audible over the music blaring from the wireless speakers I had all over the house. Some female rocker voice, fierce, unyielding, and hypnotic just like the woman who danced to it.

In nothing but an oversized T-shirt.

One that stopped just below her perfect ass.

Her long, bare legs went on for miles as she walked back and forth, piling pancakes onto a glass platter.

Fuck, I wanted to stalk behind her, palm the globes of that perfect ass, kiss the seam of her neck, flick my tongue over every inch of that glorious skin.

Dripping sweat, I knew I needed to book it to the shower, but I was frozen.

Watching her.

A line pulled taut, connecting me to her, grounding me in a way I'd never felt before.

The line continued to tug with each second I spent with her—even our cheesy date had been fun. Had left me wanting more.

More of her time.

More of her laugh.

More of *her*.

"Smells good," I finally announced myself before I reached creeper stalker territory.

She jumped, her bare feet smacking against the hardwood as she spun around. Quickly, she turned down the music and wielded the spatula at me like a weapon.

"Don't do that!"

"What?" I chuckled, the wild look in her eyes shooting straight to my dick.

Fuck she was gorgeous and funny and...*fuck*.

"Sneak up on me!" she put her free hand over her chest, catching her breath.

Cold snaked over my skin, and I realized my mistake. I crossed the distance between us in a matter of steps. "I didn't mean...shit, are you okay?"

"I'm fine," she said, waving me off. "I just don't like being snuck up on."

"Who does?"

She laughed, returning to her pancakes. "People who pay top-dollar to see horror movies, that's who." She flipped over the four rounds on the griddle, their color a perfect golden brown.

"How's the appetite?" I asked.

"Appetite is never the problem," she said, switching off the griddle and piling the last pancakes onto the platter.

"The baby *wants* to eat everything," she said. "We just regret it sometimes."

I swallowed hard, following her gaze to her tummy, and then on to the beautiful bare legs beneath it. Fuck if she let me, I'd wear those legs around my face all day long.

Lock it up.

Right.

"Hot," I said but meant it as a question.

She shifted on her feet. "It's like a sauna in here."

I tilted my head, knowing full well the thermostat had been set at sixty-two upon her arrival. "You are in front of a stove."

"Well, that didn't help either." She slid four pancakes onto a plate, then drizzled syrup all over the stack. "Want some?" she asked, eyeing my gym clothes. "You must be hungry after all that *running*." She took a small bite off the fork, her lips wrapping around the utensil in a way that made my dick twitch.

Standing there in only a t-shirt, eating right in front of the stove—fucking sexy as hell.

"I...uh..." I'd never wanted pancakes so bad in my entire life.

She *umphed* and jumped at the same time, her free hand flying to her right side. She quickly set the plate and fork down, rubbing the area behind her right hip. "You don't like pancakes, baby?"

At first, I thought she was talking to me, and the sweet tone of her voice cinched tight around my chest.

Took only a second to realize she was looking down. Holding a one-sided conversation with our unborn child.

Jealousy rippled through me when she flinched again.

I hadn't been invited to speak or feel the kicks, yet.

I shook off the sensation, moving closer to her without thinking.

"You okay?" I asked again, noting the crease between her brow.

"Yeah," she said. "Baby-ball is just getting stronger."

I reached my hands toward the spot she rubbed—not her tummy, but close enough to it that once she saw my intent, she backed *away*, almost like an instinct.

I lowered my hands, my head dropping a fraction along with my heart.

Fuck, that hurts.

Worse than a hit from Rory on the ice—and that was a mad pain like no other.

This?

Her keeping a wall between us?

Between my baby and me...*shit.*

All the air seemed to have been sucked from the room, my lungs burning for a breath worse than when I'd ran the miles this morning.

Apology flashed through her eyes, and she took a step toward me, but I backed up several feet, motioning over my shoulder with my thumb. "I've got to shower before my lunch with the guys."

"Right." Her shoulders sank, but she nodded. "Have fun."

I nodded a little too quickly, booking it down the hallway and to my shower.

Technically it was Jeannine's shower now, but I hadn't moved my stuff over to the guest bathroom yet.

I would...later. Right now, I needed ice cold water, and some damn sense knocked into me.

What had I been thinking?

That I'd move her in and she'd magically invite me into a heart she kept locked tighter than a vault?

That all it would take was me winning a stupid carnival toy for her to see I could be trusted?

That I could be a good father?

"Ridiculous," I grumbled to myself as I stepped under the cool water.

The sting hit my skin and shocked some breath into my lungs. I scrubbed and rinsed in a fierce rush, my muscles protesting the lack of warmth and length of the soak.

I couldn't linger, though, not when every second I stood in there I thought about what Jeannine looked like in this exact same spot. Nothing to hide her gorgeous body, the one now growing our child inside it.

The glow she emanated, even before she got pregnant.

The way her skin was soft like silk. I bet the hot water only made it more supple, tender, sensitive. I would use the slickness of the water to drench between her thighs, tease and torture her sweet spot until she couldn't stand on her own anymore. Until I had to hold her up while I devoured every glorious inch of her...

And, fuck me, I was hard.

Damn this woman.

Dead set on shutting me out, and could I really blame her? She'd only known one version of me.

Hell, *I* was still getting used to this new outlook...this new importance pulsing in my blood, demanding me to alter my vision of the future and *provide*.

I fisted my rock-hard dick, leaning my other arm against the shower wall. So much for a cold shower, even it had no chance against the powerhouse that was Jeannine. Those bare legs, that stunning smile. The way she owned herself and wouldn't give an inch.

That *mouth*.

Fuck.

I pumped harder, tightening my fist, seeing nothing but *her*.

The smell of her shampoo and the body wash she used that left a fresh scent on her skin was all around me, tempting me, taunting me.

Mine.

But just out of reach.

Harder.

I could almost *feel* her—my memory branded with the sensation of how it had felt to sink into her with nothing between us. The warmth of her perfect cunt, tightening and swirling around my dick. The way she'd met every single one of my animalistic thrusts—this wild woman loving it hard and fast, teasing and torturing.

I upped my pace, punishing myself for not being strong enough to withstand her fire.

Not being able to give her exactly what she needed.

For not having a clue what that really was.

From the tension in her body a moment ago, it looked like she needed exactly *this*.

Fuck me, that did it.

The image of her fingers plunging between her own thighs, exploring herself, finding the release she desperately needed...it brought on my own, and I groaned.

A few ragged breaths and I re-cleaned up, shutting the water off several minutes later. Dressed in a fresh pair of jeans and T, I both hoped she would and wouldn't be in the kitchen when I left. I wanted to see her, talk to her, try to figure out what she *really* wanted from me, but I was terrified of actually finding out the answer.

Because I was almost certain it had nothing to do with *me*.

———

A half hour later—after I sadly didn't run into Jeannine again, the kitchen clean and empty—I sank into a chair across from the guys at our favorite burger joint.

"I didn't realize this was bring-your-kid-to-lunch day," I said, glaring at Bentley who sat on Gage's left. Rory across from him and on my right.

"Crazy that you'll actually be able to do that soon, huh, old man?" Bentley fired back, and though I instantly gave the dude props for the quip, I deepened my glare.

Gage smacked the kid's chest, which was more defined than when I had left. Maybe he really had been working his ass off as much as Gage said, but that wouldn't be proven until I saw him on the ice.

"You told him?" I growled, my eyes darting between my boys.

Gage's shoulders sank. "He overheard Bailey and me talking before we came here."

"Look," Bentley said, raising his hand toward me. "I'm sorry, all right. I can't control my mouth sometimes."

I snorted, rolling my eyes.

"I meant to say congratulations." His eyes said he was being sincere, but I was still pissed he knew something so deeply personal to me. Not that I was trying to hide it, but damn, I hadn't fully adjusted yet.

"Thanks," I said but it sounded more like a growl.

Our waitress came over to the table, smiling. "The usual today guys?" She glanced around at each of us.

Rory shook his head first. "No, Suze," he said. "We're going to need whiskey today."

Her eyebrows rose, but she nodded. "Before or after burgers?"

"Both." Rory and Gage said at the same time.

She nodded and hurried off to put in our orders and grab the drinks.

"So," Gage said after a few too many minutes of silence where I sized Bentley up, and he did his best not to look me in the eye. He studied the drink menu extremely hard. "How is the houseguest?"

Beautiful.

Fun.

Infuriating.

"Fine," I said, shrugging. "Was cooking earlier without getting sick, so that is progress."

"That is a good sign," Rory said, sympathy coloring his eyes. Wasn't too long ago that he'd been in the same boat. Gage a few months ahead of him. "I bet she's going nuts not working," he continued.

I nodded, wrapping my fingers around the glass of whiskey Suze set before me. "I'm sure she is," I said, trying like hell not to sound jaded.

"Do you two...talk?" Gage asked, quickly taking a sip of his whiskey.

I took a good long pull before I answered. "Sure," I said. "We even went on a date."

"Warren Kinley went on a date?" Rory raised his eyebrows. "Did hell just freeze over?"

Bentley laughed but shut it down after a second.

I chuckled. "Yeah," I said. "Wasn't as bad as I remembered."

The last date I'd been on had been years ago, so far back

I could barely remember. The one thing I *did* remember was how it didn't fit my mold—the one relationship for life type. I'd never met a girl who could handle my dry sense of humor, or my brooding moods when I was in the zone for hockey season.

But now? There was something about Jeannine that made me re-think that thought process. Like if there was anyone that could handle me for longer than a few nights, it was her. With all her fire and attitude and strength. Who better to help keep me in check? And I'd thought *that* before I'd seen her swollen with my child.

Seeing her that way...fuck, it only made it worse.

"Where did you go?" Bentley asked, the question timid as he *tried*.

Okay, kid, I get it. You want to be in the group.

I took a breath, ensuring the snarl was gone from my voice. "A carnival."

"Oh nice," he said, nodding as he sipped his whiskey. "Chloe used to love the rubber duck game," he said, then his eyes widened like he hadn't meant to utter those words. "You play it?" He asked quickly.

I tilted my head toward Gage, who shrugged.

"No," I said. "Who's Chloe?"

"No one," he answered too fast.

I arched a brow at him. "I worked with a Chloe in Canada," I said, never losing his gaze. He flinched. "She was the Canadian trainer. Best trainer I've ever had, actually."

A muscle in his jaw ticked.

"Not the same woman, though, right?"

He sighed, content not to answer.

Oh, this was too much fun. I leaned closer, lowering my voice.

"You know about my baby mama," I said, trying not to laugh. "You can't answer a simple question?"

He stared into his glass like he wanted to dive into it and hide. "She's just an ex-girlfriend. No big deal." He forced a shrug. "She liked the carnival game. Made me think of it."

The fact that he *didn't* confirm it *wasn't* the same Chloe I'd worked with was answer enough. Fucking hell, she was everything over there in the hockey world. How'd he let that one go?

Rory pressed his lips together, Gage locked his jaw, and I simply sighed.

You could tell by the way he said her name there was some real pain there. And here he was, befriending two men hopelessly in love with their women, and me with a baby on the way. Still, he didn't throw trash talk over us being whipped...had to respect that.

"We shot guns and darts and did the hammer thing," I said, thinking of the purple puppy she'd demanded I sleep with. The thing was on the guest bed I currently occupied, not that I'd held it while I slept or anything.

"Nice," was all that Bentley managed before he cleared his throat. "So," he said. "Speaking of the Canadians. They tripled your size." He eyed me, and we all laughed.

"Checking out my muscles, Rookie?"

"What? Ugh. No, man, I just meant it looks like their system really worked for you."

"So you're saying I *needed* it?"

He opened and closed his mouth a few times. The fact that he wasn't firing back as fast as he used to earned him even more respect from me. I could see why the guys were taking him under their wing—he wasn't behaving like the hot-head rookie who wanted Gage's spot when injury threatened to take him off the team. No, this kid...something had clicked for him. Made him understand the value of having us be in his corner instead of pounding him against it.

He dropped his hands on the table. "I can't win."

Me, Rory, and Gage burst out laughing. I reached across the table and shoved his shoulder before sitting back down. "You're all right, Rookie."

His eyes darted between us all, confused as hell.

"Olympics were good. Getting the Bronze was amazing. Surreal. Spending time coaching at the Pro-skills camp was incredible, too. It was all great." I continued. Minus the phone blip that left me clueless as to what Jeannine was going through, it had been a great experience. "Like I said, Chloe taught me a few new tricks," I said, hating that his eyes shut briefly when I said her name. Fuck, poor guy. I leaned back in my seat as Suze sat down our baskets of burgers and fries. "I'll teach you a few next pick-up game."

"Really?" Bentley asked, his eyes clearing as he reached for his burger.

I chuckled. "Sure, Rookie."

Gage smiled at me, pride beaming from him.

Thanks, Dad. I silently, sarcastically told him.

"You know," Bentley said. "I've been on the team for two seasons now. I'm not exactly a rookie anymore."

Ah, there was some of that attitude I remembered him for.

"I do have a name," he continued.

I laughed. "You'll always be a rookie to me, kid."

He rolled his eyes but took it in silence.

Two more whiskeys and an empty basket later, the kid grabbed a cab home under the guise of needing to get some shit done. In all fairness, I think he wanted to give me some time with the guys without him.

If he wasn't careful, I was actually going to like him.

I ordered another drink, swirling the ice around the amber liquid.

"Carnival was on the list?" Rory asked.

"Yup."

"I bet that was Bailey," Gage said, a smile he only had when he said Bailey's name on his lips.

"What's up next?" Rory asked.

I chuckled, taking another sip. "You two are as bad as the girls."

"What?" Rory acted offended. "I've already been through my list," he said. "And a few others." A mischievous smile flashed, and I shuddered—Paige and Bailey both were like my sisters now.

"Dude, TMI," I said, laughing.

He rolled his eyes. "I can't help but be curious about yours."

"It's not anything like yours was," I said.

Or, I supposed it wasn't.

He never went into full details of what exactly was on Paige's, but he'd said enough to know it wasn't carnival's and chick-flick nights.

Funny, because the dirty kinky stuff I could handle without flinching, but having to plan dates? I was as nervous as a teenage boy seeing a girl naked for the first time.

"How are you holding up with all the other stuff?" Gage asked.

I played dumb.

He didn't buy it. "The living with a woman thing?" he asked. "A woman pregnant with your child, no less."

"It's...complicated."

"That's an understatement," Rory said.

"I can't explain it guys," I said, sighing. "I couldn't stop thinking about her *before* I found out."

They both raised their brows at that, and I nodded.

"It's true," I said. "Why did you think I didn't come home with even *one* phone number? I wanted her so much I couldn't even *try* to sleep with anyone else."

Rory spit whiskey across the table, misting Gage.

"Dude, what the fuck?" Gage swiped the stuff off his shirt.

"Sorry, man, but holy fuck," he said by way of apology. "You didn't sleep with anyone for six months?"

I shook my head, wondering why I hated that it was such a shock. I used to pride myself on the women I bedded —all wonderful, consenting encounters with no strings.

Now, I wished I could change it.

Lessen it.

So that what Jeannine and I had shared, even for just that one night, would be more...profound somehow.

"Damn," Gage said, flipping Rory off when he passed him a napkin.

"But it doesn't matter," I said. "She doesn't want anything to do with me. Not yet. Not beyond a place to stay and the list."

"That can't be true," Gage said.

"Yeah," Rory agreed. "She wouldn't move in with you if she didn't trust you."

The vision of her flinching away from my touch begged to differ.

I raked my fingers through my hair.

"It'll take time," Gage said. "She's been on her own forever."

"Paige said she's been taking care of herself since she

was sixteen," Rory added. "Her family life is foggy. Paige's family became *her* family."

"Right," I said. "I get it. She needs time."

"Just, don't give up," Gage said. "All right?"

I shook my head, ensuring him I wouldn't.

But as we finished our whiskey, I couldn't help but think about how *little* time I had before she disappeared.

And took my baby along with her.

CHAPTER 7

JEANNINE

"THIS IS *SO* BAILEY," I said, grinning as Warren pulled me into the Seattle Aquarium.

"I would think so," he said. "But it's all in Paige's handwriting, so it's kind of a fun game to guess."

"I'll remember that on the next one," I said.

The next one.

I couldn't believe I had a number of more dates with Warren. This was only our second, but I found myself excited for each one.

It wasn't like me at all—usually, I was so focused on work and expanding my menu options or whatnot that I found *stopping to smell the roses* trivial. I couldn't have been more wrong. These past couple days with Warren had been like the vacation I'd never had, and while I was still guarded emotionally—for both the baby and my sake—I was happy.

Except for when I thought about how'd I'd flinched away from his touch last week.

Then I was mortified.

I hadn't meant to...it just happened on reflex. A survival mechanism. Something I knew stemmed from my own absentee family. I would not do that to my child, and I wouldn't allow anyone else to, either. While Warren was currently making me happy and doing all he could to prove himself, I knew once the Shark's season started everything would change.

I had to *keep* reminding myself of this every time I felt myself relaxing a little too much in his presence.

Warren's hand rested effortlessly in mine, the action becoming so expected it was natural by now. The contact felt better than I'd admit, and whenever he did that thing where he traced the lines on my palm and wrist, I practically melted.

"This is beautiful," I said, walking up to the first giant saltwater tank on the right. The thing was massive, rising all the way to the ceiling. The gorgeous blue water only made the neon colors of the fish pop as they meandered back and forth.

"It really is," he said, and I glanced his way. He was looking right at me but quickly averted his gaze to the fish. "Nemo." He pointed to the small clownfish, swallowing hard.

"Good eyes." Heat flushed my body.

How were we nervous around each other?

I was carrying his child for Christ's sake.

Maybe that was the reason.

Or maybe it was because of our insanely unique situation. Or it was because I wasn't used to this new side of Warren. The one who floundered, the one who had vulnerability in those normally cocky eyes, the one who'd reached for my tummy yesterday and I'd pulled away.

Guilt ate at my insides.

Yes, I was terrified.

Terrified of letting myself feel for him.

Anything—friendly, more than friendly. It was all a slippery slope, one I didn't want to put on the baby. It wasn't just my heart that would get crushed if I fell for a guy who wasn't commitment ready to put us ahead of his career.

Again, not that I could blame him. He didn't ask for this. Neither did I, but I owned it in a way that claimed my soul. I would be enough for this baby. I would be everything.

Warren led me around the aquarium, stopping to admire each tank with an aloofness that set me at ease. Like there really wasn't any place he'd rather be, as he'd said the other day at the carnival.

"Oh my," I said as I followed him into a large tunnel-like walkway. The entire room was surrounded by glass, even the ceiling. A variety of fish swam lazily over the ceiling and down past the walls surrounding us. "Look at this guy!" I hurried to the right side, pointing to a giant sea turtle that moved through the water with such easy, fluid movements.

"Damn, he's big." Warren leaned next to me as we got closer to the glass.

I nodded, watching him swim.

So this is what normal people do on dates.

Go to cool places, see cool stuff, content to simply be together.

I could get used to it.

But I shouldn't.

Right. Because Warren wouldn't be around forever. He was only doing this now to prove he was capable of it, not to show he was in it for life.

Well, I can at least enjoy it while it lasts.

A five-foot bull shark darted past the glass, jolting me. I stumbled backward, but two strong hands caught my hips to steady me.

"Whoa, there," he said, smiling down at me. "I thought you weren't afraid of Sharks."

My heart raced in my chest from the surprise guest, but it increased due to Warren's touch. He was so close I could smell him—delicious, spicy, man.

"Only when they surprise me," I said, trying to calm my breathing.

"Learned that the hard way," he said, no doubt remembering the episode in the kitchen. The same one where I pulled away. I needed to amend that as soon as possible. This baby was as much his as it was mine, I just couldn't help protecting it with everything I had.

"Oh!" I flinched, the baby-ball using a karate chop move on my ribs—like it was scolding me for remembering my blunder. I palmed the left side of my round stomach, my brow scrunched.

"What is it?" Warren asked, his eyes darting from my face to my hand. "Do you need to sit? Should I call the doctor?"

The panic in his features melted my heart.

This beast of a man—solid like he was carved out of marble, with dark eyes fierce enough to steal breath—was worried about us. About me.

"No," I said. "The baby is just trying to be like you, I think."

He swallowed hard. "What?"

"Strong. The thing has a mean kick."

Warren laughed, and the baby-ball kicked again.

My heart thumped hard against my chest, threatening to climb up my throat as I reached for Warren's hand. I'd pushed him away last week, but I'd been taken off guard.

I was in control, now, and I *wanted* him to feel this.

To give this piece of myself to him.

"Here," I said, guiding his trembling hand to where the baby kicked like a ninja who had too many Redbulls.

He wetted his lips, his eyes both unsure and excited as I held his huge hand on the spot on my tummy.

I held my breath, waiting.

Nothing.

Warren's eyes flashed up to mine, and I hated the defeat I saw there.

"Laugh again."

"What?" He asked. "I can't laugh on command."

I rolled my eyes, keeping his hand firmly in place. "Picture Rory skating in a tutu."

He glowered at me.

"Picture Gage taking a shot in a feather boa and a tiara."

Nothing.

"Ugh, fine. Picture them both wearing that and being attacked by bees on the ice."

Warren laughed, shaking his head.

Kick. Kick. Kick.

His laughter died, replaced with a gasp.

He laughed again, this one a little forced but more in awe.

Kick. Kick.

I watched his eyes glued to the area where I held his hand. They glittered just slightly.

"I can feel you, baby," he said, the tone so soft I may not have heard it if I hadn't been so close. He finally looked at me. "It's incredible."

"Baby-ball likes your laugh. Go figure."

It was a hell of a laugh.

One that made me weak.

"You keep calling it baby-ball," he said.

"Yes," I said, releasing his hand, allowing him to rub it over my belly. "It looks like a perfect ball, doesn't it?"

"Perfect." He slowly reached toward me with his other hand, but flickered his eyes to me in question, like he was afraid I would run away again.

I nodded, swallowing the emotions in my throat as he set his other hand on the opposite side of my belly.

I sighed at the contact, the way his warmth seeped into my skin and filled me in ways no innocent touch should. A deep hunger roared to life, as it often did around Warren, and I found myself out of control of my breathing again.

"Are you all right?" He asked, never letting me go.

"Mmmhmm," I mumbled, wishing I could find the voice I was so sure of a moment ago.

"You don't know the sex, do you?"

For a moment, all I heard was *sex*.

Yes, please.

"Wait," I said, blinking out of my lust filled haze. "What?"

"Do you know if it's a boy or a girl?"

I shook my head. "I wanted to be surprised."

He smiled. "I love that."

The moment was charged and yet soft.

Aching hunger and yet filled.

Hot damn, the man made my head spin.

Made my heart wish for things I knew weren't possible.

But for the moment, I was content in the chaos. I would soak this up for as long as I could because I couldn't remember a time when I'd felt so...cared for.

"You hungry, baby?" He asked, and for a moment I thought he was talking to me again, but he was looking at my tummy, and it somehow made it much more adorable.

Kick. Kick. Kick.

Oh my gosh, baby-ball you're already starting banter with your father?

Father.

Dangerously close to losing my mind.

"Do we have lunch plans?" I asked, clearing my voice when it cracked.

Warren straightened, releasing my stomach only to take my hand.

"We do." He pointed up with his free hand.

I arched a brow. "We're eating with the fishes?"

"Sort of."

An elevator ride later, we were seated in a private dining room on the roof. Floor-to-ceiling windows over-looked the city and a stunning tank with some of the most gorgeous fish I'd ever seen inside made up one of the restaurant walls.

I opened the menu, nodding at the simple yet elegant style. "You sure know how to wine and dine a girl," I said, tilting my head. "Minus the wine."

He chuckled. "How hard has that been?"

"What, not drinking?" I asked.

"Yeah," he said, setting down his menu.

"Not as hard as you'd think." I gave our waitress my order and turned back to him. "After I saw those two pink lines, everything *shifted*. Like everything that had been before that moment crumbled inside me, only to rebuild in a way that made me stronger, protective, loving. Sure, I was terrified, but I was also filled with this insane sense of purpose. I miss wine. Trust me. But it's not so bad. The hardest thing has honestly been the worrying."

"About..."

I puffed out a breath. "Everything."

I laughed and he laughed and the baby-ball kicked.

"About the baby being healthy," I continued. "About me being a good mom, about something happening during labor and me being alone." The last part slipped out, and I quickly took a drink of water to try and swallow *that* truth.

"Your mom?" he asked.

I shook my head, figuring Rory and Gage had already filled him on my family history. But he was kind enough to pretend like they didn't. To give me the choice to open up about a past I'd rather forget.

"My parents haven't been in the picture for a long time," I said, the moment charged between us. Because that fact that I wanted to tell him, that I trusted him enough with this darkness...it meant everything. "They're not dead or anything. Well, not in the technical sense of the word." I glanced down, my throat tightening as memories flooded me. "I won't go into detail, but I wouldn't attend their funeral even if they were." I swallowed hard. "We're not a family. Paige became that when I was sixteen and then Bailey later."

"And you don't want the girls in the room?" He asked, and I breathed a sigh, so damn grateful he didn't press for gory details of my past. Or looked at me any differently.

"Not really, no. I've always done things on my own," I said, sighing. "Plus, I don't mind if they're there, but there are only so many things a best friend can do. It's not like having—" I stopped mid-sentence, blaming my hormones for my total lack of filter.

Warren furrowed his brow as our waitress set our orders down. "Like what?" He asked after she'd left.

"It's not important."

"Nine," he chided. "It is. I can tell." He pushed his steak around his plate. "Look, I know we're still getting used to this new situation between us, and I know I'm not your ideal candidate for a partner, but I want you to talk to me. I want to be what you need. What the baby needs. So...talk."

Heat flushed my body.

"Okay," I said. "I've had plenty of time to think about this. Six months is a long time to be on your own and reevaluate your choices. I would never, not for a second, take this back," I said. "And that doesn't mean *you* have to feel that way. I'd totally get it if you regret what happened, but I don't. And I'm fine with that. I'm fine with being a single mother. I know I can do it."

"But," he said, waving me on to continue.

"But," I said. "With all that time to think, I had plenty of time to think about what it would be like if we'd...*I'd* done things in the normal way. You know, date. Relationship, marriage, *then* baby." I chuckled. "At least when you're married, you'd have that person in the room with you telling you you're gorgeous even though you likely look like a swamp creature. And they'd be there to take care of the hard things—like paperwork and legal decisions—afterward when you're too tired to think straight." I sighed. "I think about these things, worry about them. How I'll handle all the tough choices...after the big push."

Warren had frozen with a piece of steak on his fork.

"I'm sorry," I said quickly. "Not really dinner talk."

"It's fine," he said, setting his bite down. "Honestly. I hadn't thought that far ahead."

"How far have you thought?"

He chuckled. "Tonight?"

I laughed, taking a bite of a decent piece of grilled chicken.

"I'm more worried about earning a spot in your life than I have been about the future."

Well, that was an honest answer.

"You're not doing so bad," I said, grinning after another bite.

"Yeah?" He smirked.

That paired with the sincerity in his eyes hit every *fuck-me-now* button I had.

The buttons had tripled since I'd gotten pregnant.

I held my palm out and down, shaking it back and forth. "So-so," I amended.

"What could I do to increase my chances?"

Kiss me until I shake.

Touch me where I can't reach.

Shatter me.

I blinked a few times, forcing myself out of the past where Warren had made my body *his*. "Date number two is a win," I said, ignoring the question altogether.

"Things would go a lot smoother if you'd tell me exactly what you wanted."

"You're doing great on your own," I assured him. "Besides," I said. "I don't know if you could handle exactly what I want."

And I could never ask.

Please serve me with multiple orgasms?

Come on.

I was huge, pregnant, and had no clue how to navigate that road. This is why married people didn't realize how lucky they were. They could have sex without having to ask for it, without having to wonder *how* to admit how badly they wanted that connection again.

How desperately I crave to be intimate with the person who gave me the greatest gift I never knew I wanted.

Warren reached for my hand across the table, taking it in his, lazily tracing those lines until I trembled inside. "I told you before," he said, his dark eyes pinning mine. "I can handle you."

A warm shiver rolled up my spine.

Could he?

Could he tell how badly I wanted him?

Could he sense it on me?

"Well," I said, my voice barely a whisper. "If the time comes where I'm ready to tell you exactly what I want...I will. Trust me."

"Fair enough." He nodded and pulled his hand back to keep eating. After a few bites, he smirked at me again. "I'll be waiting."

CHAPTER 8

WARREN

A LITTLE OVER SEVEN MONTHS.

Two left to go.

And Jeannine still hadn't told me exactly what she wanted, despite me checking off a few more items from her list the past month.

I didn't mind it—the dates. Each one was better than the next, but simply being around her was fun. Even if we ordered in, even if she randomly fell asleep on the couch during a show, even if she continued to torture me with those fleeting looks where I swore she wanted more.

But I'd never push her.

She'd come to me when she was ready.

I'd just have to continue giving her every reason to trust me.

And find a replacement for cold showers because those sure as shit weren't doing anything against my need for that woman.

Smack!

Rory slammed me into the boards, my helmet bouncing

off the partition, effectively cutting off all thoughts of Jeannine.

"Where you at, Kinley?" Rory quipped, skating backward as he taunted.

I shook off the hit, noting the move had freed up Gage to get the puck from Bentley, who, to his credit, was trying like hell to get it back for us.

Gage had paired me with the rookie to test us both.

We were getting along just fine until I'd been distracted by all things Nine.

"Fuck me," I snarled, skating after Rory.

He laughed. "That is the problem, isn't it?"

"You will pay for that, Jackson!" I hollered despite being on his heels. I had no cares for the puck anymore—I only wanted to destroy Rory.

"Don't hate me because I speak truth," he pumping up his speed. I matched him skate for skate until I finally caught the prick. "Umph!" He jolted as I shoved him into the boards behind the goal.

The open goal that Gage easily slid the puck into.

It won them the pick-up game we'd started a couple of hours ago.

"Damn!" Bentley snapped. It looked like he wanted to throw his stick against the ice, but he reeled it in. Slowly skating to Gage, he glove-bumped him. "Good game, man."

I raised my brows as I helped Rory up. The kid had gotten a lock on the anger—no easy feat for any of us. Impressive.

"Thanks," Rory said, fully standing now. "That was one hell of a hit."

"You deserved it."

He laughed. "Don't I always?"

We headed to the locker room, shedding our gear in a

lazy sort of way before each of us hitting separate showers. Once we'd gathered back near our lockers, fresh clothes on, Rory kept eyeing me from where he sat.

"What's on your mind, Jackson?" I finally asked, even though I was pretty sure I knew where his head was at.

He debated for a few seconds before shrugging. "Wondering how things are going."

I kept my lips in a line, my jaw locked.

"From the force behind the hit and the way you were distracted, I'm guessing not so good?"

Gage glanced between us as he shucked his bag to the floor, and sat next to Rory.

"It's not going bad," I admitted. "We spend almost every day together."

"And you're...over it?" Gage asked.

"No," I said quickly. "Not at all. She's the most fun person, even when she's in a hormonal rage because there is no ice cream left in the house." I chuckled to myself, remembering her rant a couple of weeks ago as she stomped through the house grumbling about the lack of her favorite treat. I'd calmed her by showing her the deep freeze in the garage where I'd stockpiled a dozen pints.

"So what's the problem?"

I raked my fingers through my hair. The pick-up game had been just what I needed—a workout for my overly tense body. Sorting out frustrations on the ice had always been my go-to when life became stressful, but the guy-talk after? Not exactly what I was looking for.

My boys always knew how to cut to the quick with me, which was why I'd avoided them for the past month. They were my brothers, but I wasn't ready to admit how terrified I was of what was happening between Jeanine and me.

Or not happening.

"It's cool, Warren," Gage said. "You don't have to talk to us. We've just been there before. And I remember being a chaotic mess up here," he said, tapping his temple. "And I wouldn't have shaken it if you two hadn't talked some sense into me."

Rory nodded in agreement.

"Right," I said. "I get that. And I was happy to be there for each of you, but this is so drastically different from falling for your best friend," I said, glancing at Gage. "And then losing your mind over a woman who needed your help," I continued and eyed Rory. "What happened to us is so damn backward, not that I regret it."

Which was the damn truth.

I never knew I wanted this until she showed up at the rink that day spitting fire and looking incredible carrying my child.

Even if given the choice, I wouldn't go back in time and put a condom on.

"I don't think she wants more from me. Even after these last few weeks—which have been the best of my life—she hasn't opened fully to me, yet."

"You can't give up," Rory said the words he'd said to me a hundred times before.

"I'm not." I glanced at both of them, watching as Bentley rounded the corner. He stopped suddenly as he surveyed the serious looks between the three of us.

"My bad," he said, hands raised as he hurried to his locker. "Grab my shit and be out of here." He rushed through the process, and I flashed the rookie a smile as he waved goodbye.

"He's changed," I said, nodding. "I hate to say it, but I might actually like him."

Gage laughed. "Told you."

They fell silent.

Patient.

Waiting.

Fucking hell.

"I think I'm falling for her."

There.

I said it.

Something I'd never said before in my life.

"I think I'm in love with her," I continued like it needed clarification.

"You have to tell her," Gage said on the end of a sigh. He knew how deep of a situation this was, how delicate. That was the bonus of the guys knowing Jeannine—they knew how independent she was, how she'd never wanted to have to rely on someone before.

And I didn't want her to *just* rely on me—I knew she'd be fine without me. She'd be an amazing mother regardless if I was in her life or not.

But I wanted her to have the *choice*.

The option to ask for help.

Or for me to simply give it to her without her needing to speak it. That is what I'd been trying to do these last weeks, but I never wanted to cross a line with her. Never wanted to push her too far too soon, so terrified she'd run scared.

"Before it gets deeper," Rory added, all of us rising, ready to get the hell out of the locker room where all the heavy had landed.

"Right," I said. "If I could just figure out a way to do that without her thinking I'm only saying it because of the baby."

Rory arched a brow as we headed toward the doors.

"You *know* it's not just the baby," I said, glaring at him.

"We know," Gage said, holding the door open for us.

"I just like to fuck with you, man," Rory said. "We could tell that first day you were back. You should've been spouting off about your Canada conquests. Instead, you didn't say a word. You did everything you could to avoid asking us about Jeannine. We knew then."

"Glad you two did," I said, following them out. "Took me a bit longer."

"Hard to change a lifetime of habits in a matter of seconds," Gage said.

"That's true." I nodded as we made it down the hallway. "For Nine too—"

"Warren Kinley," a sugary sweet, slightly familiar female voice called as we rounded the corner toward the exit to the parking lot. "You're a hard man to find!" The tease in her voice brought her face to my mind, and I cringed as I slowly turned, finding her leaning near the glass doors.

Shay Morgan.

Petite, brunette, puck bunny.

A line I'd never crossed because she was *too* invested—farther than wearing my number on her back, but showing up to places no one knew I'd be. That, and I'd caught her more times than I could count being hateful to other fans. That shit didn't fly with me.

Didn't matter, she constantly tried to change my mind.

"We'll wait for you outside," Rory said, both guys flashing me a *good luck* look.

I resisted the urge to flip them both off for leaving me hanging. Instead, I gripped my gear bag on my shoulder a little tighter.

"How's it going, Shay?" I asked, trying for polite but coming out a bit irritated.

I'd been cordial, and denied her in the best way I

possibly could, but she kept coming back. Rory had learned the hard way to never cross the line with puck bunnies that were stalker level, and I would not repeat his mistake. Of course, everything had worked out in the end, but Linda had nearly destroyed his and Paige's relationship.

"Better now that you're back." She practically purred as she swished her hips, spanning the distance between us in a matter of strides. Reaching toward me, she trailed her red-polished fingers over my chest. "Olympics were fun, I take it?"

I took a step back, her hand hovering in the space where I'd been before she dropped it. She narrowed her gaze but kept that too sweet smile on her face, the one that never reached her eyes.

Fuck, why does the rink have to be lax in the offseason?

Usually, my driver would've run interference for me and warned me of anything like this before I came out of the room. But I always gave him time off when we weren't playing.

"You want to get a drink?" she asked, pushing her chest out, the low cut v-neck shirt showing off her cleavage.

Not even a flicker.

A twitch.

Nothing.

I hadn't had sex in seven months and not even a flash of heat.

Before, I knew I'd never sleep with her, but I'd at least been able to appreciate her looks, whether she looked at me like a piece of meat or not.

Now?

Nothing thrummed in my blood.

Nothing urged me to rush out and find a suitable

woman for the night who had the same plans as me—no strings, just fun, all good.

"No thanks," I said, turning toward the exit. "I'm actually meeting someone in a few. Have a good one!" I called over my shoulder, high-tailing it out there before she could try to sink her claws into me. I knew I was a conquest to her, nothing more, and that never bothered me. But now that everything had changed, I didn't want to linger for one second too long. I knew from Rory's experiences that it only took a picture to crush a heart.

I would never let that happen to Nine.

And we weren't even dating.

Holy fuck, I really am in love with her.

Rory and Gage leaned against my car, their bags already stored in their own cars.

"How'd that go?" Rory asked.

"Fine." I shrugged. "I kind of hoped being away would've cooled the bunny interest."

"Never going to happen," Gage said, pointing at his wedding ring. "I've been wearing this since we got engaged. They still come around."

"It's true," Rory said. "Some of them, more so."

"How did you deal with it?" I asked him. "You've had it worst."

"Yeah," Gage cut in. "Why do you think that is?"

"That I've had more puck bunny stalker drama than you two?" Rory asked.

We both nodded.

He rolled his eyes. "Duh," he said. "It's because I'm prettier than the pair of you."

Gage and I dropped our jaws in mock shock.

"You're definitely the most high-maintenance out of all of us," I said.

"You do love to preen in front of the mirror for hours on end." Gage laughed.

He flipped us both off. "You want my advice or not?"

I cleared my throat and waved my hand at him. "Lay it on me."

"Don't let them come near you," he said.

"Well, thanks. That helps a ton. Especially in cases like just now where I can't help it."

"I know. But take precautions. Check the place out before you go in—wherever that is. Or stay in."

"That sounds a lot like letting them control my life."

Rory shrugged. "You don't have to live that way...if..."

"If what?"

He clamped his hand on my shoulder. "You *tell* her she's the only one for you. Tell her you love her. Then let her know about the bunnies and the lengths they go to get a taste."

The notion shot ice-cold terror through my blood. "And if I'm not ready?"

Rory patted my shoulder, releasing me. "Then you become a hermit."

"Brilliant."

Gage flashed me a sympathetic look. "Sounds easier to fess up."

"Yeah, and send her running the opposite direction because I'm not what she wants."

"You don't know that."

"I know," I said. "But I *feel* it." I fished my keys out of my pocket. "Anyway," I said, a pathetic transition to end the discussion. "Thanks for the pickup game." I laughed. "And the pep-talk."

"Anytime," Rory said, heading to his car.

"You know it," Gage added, turning the opposite direction toward his.

As I sank behind the wheel of mine, I let out a heavy sigh. The last thing I wanted was for some picture to surface —past or future—that would paint me in a compromising position with a bunny.

Not if it would hurt Jeannine.

I would do anything to keep that from happening.

Even become a hermit.

Lucky for me, I had a seven months pregnant roommate who often grumbled when I suggested an outing.

The image of her pout set my blood on fire, shooting straight to my dick.

Fuck, the woman was fully pregnant with my child, and she was the sexist person I'd ever laid eyes on.

And I'm in love with her.

And she doesn't have a clue.

Maybe it was time to tell her.

If I can't?

Then maybe I could *show* her.

CHAPTER 9

JEANNINE

"YOU TWO ARE THE BEST," I said as Paige pulled into Warren's driveway.

"I'm just shocked the man let you out of the house," Bailey teased from the backseat.

"Truth," Paige said, parking in front of our house...*his* house.

Shit, when did I start thinking of it as ours?

"Y'all are one to talk! You two rarely leave your houses besides for work." I teased.

"A ten-month-old and a fourteen-month-old are kind of a handful," Paige said, laughing.

"Excuses." I dramatically rolled my eyes. I'd gotten some good Ethan and Daphne time before Gage's mom showed up to watch them during our shopping trip—Lettie was busy with kindergarten.

"Warren is taking the list and the pregnancy seriously," Paige continued like I hadn't made the joke.

I shifted in the passenger seat so I could see them both. "I know."

Bailey's eyes lit up, and Paige flashed me a *told-you-so* look.

"I know," I said again, and this time I couldn't help but smile.

"And we know you've been having fun on these dates he's taken you on every week," Bailey said, fishing again.

They'd been after me throughout our girl's day, digging for intel on what happened between Warren and myself when the lights went out.

The truth was...nothing.

And it was getting harder.

It was like I could practically *feel* the incredibly strong, sex-god-of-a-Shark sleeping in the room across the hall. He was so close, yet so far, and I hated that I wanted him as close to me as humanly possible.

"We've been on six dates," I said. "And, yes, I'm just as shocked as you two that I've enjoyed them."

That much was true. I'd never been the overly-romantic-date girl. Never had the time to fall *heart* first into a relationship in order for there to be dates like the ones Warren had crossed off the list. But, with him literally anything was fun—even the brunch and antique mall had been a blast.

"See," Paige said. "With the right person—"

"He makes me laugh." I cut her off before she could launch into another *Warren-might-be-the-one* speech. She and Bailey totally agreed on it after they'd seen me. They said I was glowing—happier than I'd ever been. I told them it was baby-ball, not Warren, but even I wasn't sure anymore. "And," I continued. "Even if this is all just a fantasy? A few checkmarks on a list to prove he is dependable enough to be in the baby-ball's life?" I sighed, leaning my head back against the headrest, not wanting to admit the warmth in my heart. "It's the best time I've had in..." I let the sentence hang there as I shook my head. I couldn't remember a time when I'd been happier.

"That's great!" Bailey squeezed my shoulder, and Paige nodded enthusiastically.

"Is it?" I asked. "What if the last item gets crossed off the list and I agree to let him be in our lives and he bolts? Or he wants to go back to being the playboy Shark while checking in on baby-ball on the weekends? What if we'll always be second to his career—"

"What if it's not for the sake of the list at all?" Paige cut me off. "What if he's actually trying? What if he wants this? With you?"

I swallowed hard. I'd never allowed myself to believe it could be real, no matter how much my heart whispered for it to be true.

"What if it doesn't work out?" My voice was hushed. Even with my two best friends, I was terrified of admitting how much I'd fallen for the man.

"What if it does?" Bailey challenged. "Think about it. What if it *did* work out? Would it be worth it?"

"The risk of getting hurt? The risk of hurting the baby-ball because its mom went all damsel without thinking?"

"Falling in love doesn't make you a damsel," Paige chided. "Loving someone takes a strength I'd never known."

"Truth," Bailey said.

"I never said I was in love with him." The statement was clear but the sting in my chest sharp.

Why did that feel like a lie?

"And that's okay," Bailey said. "We just don't want you to *not* explore something because you're scared or because you think it makes you weak."

Paige's eyes went from serious to sincere and back again. "You're never going to be your mother."

I sucked in a sharp breath, my eyes glittering.

One of my biggest fears—beyond that of falling for Warren and him bolting the second he went back on Shark mode—was turning out like my mother.

Which was absent.

Abusive.

Same with my dad.

They'd divorced when I was three, and I never saw him again.

And mom? Well, she blamed me for so many years, punished me for something out of my control. So, once I could, I'd left and never looked back.

Thank God for Paige and her family taking me in.

I wouldn't be where I was today without her, and a shit-ton of hard work.

"You two don't know me," I finally said, wiping under my eyes.

They laughed, both of them leaning in to give me a big hug. I shifted in the seat, opening the door.

"Just let yourself be open, Nine," Paige called as I hefted myself out of her car.

"Yeah, yeah," I said, waddling around toward the back of it. "Open myself up to rainbows and puppies. Got it. Pop the trunk."

They chuckled as I grabbed the four shopping bags that were mine out of her trunk. I bent slightly as I passed her opened passenger window. "I love you both," I said.

"See?" Bailey grinned. "That wasn't so hard, was it?"

I flipped her off and waddled to the front door. I struggled with my key for a minute as Paige drove away. Finally,

I managed to get the door open and shut without dropping a single bag.

The smell of burnt chocolate instantly hit my nose, and I hurried into the kitchen. "Whoa," I blurted as I dropped my bags on the island.

"Whoa," Warren said, eyeing the bags. A once-white apron strained at the seams over his massive chest. The fabric now covered in streaks of glistening chocolate, puffs of white flour, and well...it looked like just about every baking ingredient he had in his kitchen.

The countertops were worse than his apron, the beautiful range more-so. A stand mixer was still rotating too fast, splashing the egg-yolk-covered countertops with more chocolate batter.

"So, this is what a Shark does in the offseason," I said, nodding as I walked around the island. I flipped off the mixer, arching a brow at him.

A flash of panic burst in his eyes, and he spun around, throwing open the stove door. He reached for a pan—without a glove—and hissed. I flinched, reaching for him, but he grabbed an oven-mitt and jerked out the pan. It landed on the dirty range with a clunk. He huffed, switched off the stove, and shrugged.

"You make this shit look easy."

I burst out laughing, studying the concoction on the pan a bit closer. I glanced back at him. "You were trying to make my filo-brownie?"

"You said it was your favorite."

I scanned the disaster of a kitchen. "You did all this...for me?"

He crossed his arms over his chest. "I thought it might be a nice surprise after a long girls' day."

My heart did a damn flip which made baby-ball kick.

This beast of a man could throw me over his shoulder like I was nothing more than a party-favor—instead, he'd slipped on an apron and tried to make one of my most difficult desserts, just to surprise me?

No one had ever done anything like that for me.

Damn it; now my eyes were glittering again.

"I'm definitely surprised," I said, grinning.

"Yeah," he chuckled, bringing his burned finger closer to his face to inspect it.

"Here, let me see," I said, stepping into his space and breathing him in.

Now he smelled like him and chocolate and good *God* I was in trouble. He gave me his hand easily, and I turned it over, running my finger along the inside of his palm simply because I could. "I've had more burns and cuts and scars than I can count," I said, though my voice was a tad breathless.

"Cooking is dangerous." His voice was low, gravely.

I nodded, taking the slightly red pad of his finger and gently touching it to see if it was going to blister. He hissed, but I flashed him an *oh-please* look. It wasn't going to blister. It was barely even red anymore.

"That stings," he said.

"Poor baby Shark," I said, tsking.

"Hey—"

I dipped my mouth over the pad of the offended finger, cutting off his words. Swirling my tongue over the hurt, I glanced up at him. He'd frozen, but his eyes were wide and alert and...wanting. I sucked it before popping it out of my mouth.

"Better?" I asked, taking a tiny step back.

His Adam's apple bobbed up and down as he nodded.

"Good," I said. "That's my go-to cure. Well, for myself anyway."

Ugh, why did I do that?

The taste of his skin was still on my tongue, and I was desperate for more.

"Now," I said, grabbing a rag and wetting it at the sink. I needed to busy my hands before I did something stupid. "Let's clean this place up. Then I'll show you how to make a filo-brownie."

For a few moments, he stood there, his fierce gaze on me, his carved muscles barely moving enough for him to breathe. A battle raged in his eyes, and I couldn't tell if he wanted to kick me out or bend me over. The latter thought sent a hot shiver down my spine. I scrubbed at the counter-tops a little harder.

Finally, he moved. Not to bend me over, but to help me clean. The room was hot, and though I could blame the stove, it was hotter in the places where we brushed against each other on our way to complete another task. Like a sizzling electricity that begged to be played with.

Touched.

Or maybe it was just me, starved for him.

After a good twenty-minutes of clean up, we had the place looking perfect again. I quickly set out all the prep bowls and ingredients we'd need and lined them up on the counter near the stove.

"Pay attention," I said, happy to have found my voice again. One that didn't sound breathless and desperate for his touch.

"Oh, I am," he said, and damn him his voice was still gravely with all the good-pure-man-grit.

I explained the details while I mixed the batter, showed him how to keep the filo-dough moist as we went. And though it was something I could do with my eyes closed, I kept stumbling. Forgetting how to say something or struggling to recall the measurements.

I kept tasting his skin in my mouth.

Kept smelling the mixture of him and the chocolate.

Kept accidentally touching his muscled forearm as I reached for something.

"And, now," I said, shoving the tray of brownies into the stove. "We wait for those to get firm enough, and then we'll roll them in the dough to crisp up."

"Amazing," he said as I shut the stove and turned to lean against the counter.

I shrugged. "It's what I do."

"I know. *You're* amazing."

I shook my head, heat flushing to my cheeks like I was a damn teenager getting her first compliment. God, why did he have to make me feel so...

Happy?

Excited?

Hungry.

"How long does it take?" He asked, motioning toward the stove as he moved closer. He stood in front of me, only an inch between my belly and him.

"About forty-minutes." My voice cracked, and I spun around, busying myself with cleaning up the absolutely spotless counter. I couldn't look into those eyes without *wanting* him.

The need worse than it ever had been and I was terrified he could see it all over my face. I didn't want it to scare him, my desire, my desperation. I wanted to live in this fantasy for as long as I could.

"Jeannine," he said, the nearness of his voice indicating he hadn't budged an inch.

"Uh huh?" I answered, unhooking the bowl on the mixer, and moved past him to put it in the sink. I flicked on the faucet, allowing the dirty bowl to fill with water.

"*Nine*," he said, and the primal demand in his tone had me whirling around.

"What?" I asked, my voice a whisper.

He stalked toward me, placing one hand on the counter next to me, the other pushing back some of my hair. "I'm trying," he said.

"I know," I responded quickly. "You've been incredible—"

"I'm *trying*," he cut me off. "To wait for you. To respect what you need."

Wait for me to what?

Oh God, he wants me to tell him he's earned his place so I'll leave.

My heart sank to the pit of my stomach.

I glanced down, hiding my eyes that were filling with tears.

Fuck my life; I had never been so quick to cry...*never*. Fucking hormones.

"I understand."

He tipped my chin up, confusion furrowing his brow. "I don't think you do," he said, dropping his hand to rest on the other side of me. His strong abdomen brushed against my belly and the touch was enough to make me tremble inside. "I don't want to push you. But, woman, I've never wanted anyone as badly as I do you. I'm a strong man, but if you don't let me at least *kiss* you, I might have a fucking heart attack."

"What?" I gasped. "How could you want..." I glanced down.

I couldn't even see my feet.

He covered my lips with his finger. "Don't you dare say one bad thing about this body." He eyed me in question as he moved his hand to hover over my belly. I nodded, and he smoothed his fingers over it. I sighed at his touch. "You're the most gorgeous woman I've ever seen. Before, and now, and you will be after. The fact that you're carrying my child only makes you more stunning."

"Warren," I whispered, unable to voice a proper thank you. An explanation for how much his words touched me. I didn't realize how desperate I was to hear them until they came out of his mouth.

"If you don't want me, that's a different thing altogether," he said, running his hand up my arm and to the back of my neck. "But if you do? If there is any part of you that wants this..." he gripped my hand and moved it downward, laying it over what was rock hard in his pants.

"Oh, God," the words rushed from me upon contact. "Just a kiss?" I whispered.

I could handle just a kiss.

Just a kiss would mean I was still in control, still being smart.

"I'll take whatever you'll give me." He inched his mouth closer to mine, his strong, warm body molding around me like the sweetest sun on a cold day.

Fucking hell he's turned me into a love-struck girl.

He smoothed his nose over the line of my jaw and pressed soft kisses to my neck, behind my ear, my cheeks.

So slow.

So gentle.

This beast who growled at the tiniest hint of an argument. Who broke men on the ice for a living...was being tender with me.

The contrast was so damn maddening it made me dizzy.

And he *watched* me.

His dark eyes never left my face, gauging my reaction as he tested these new waters.

The Shark handled me like I was *precious*.

Each gentle, almost feather-light caress drew a heavy sigh from my lips. My entire body buzzed, ached, and *hummed* for him.

His lips finally grazed mine, just a breath of a touch, and I whimpered.

Then he claimed my mouth like the Shark I remembered from seven months ago.

He sucked my tongue into his mouth, rubbing it with his own. Flicked it over the edges of my teeth, the sensitive spot on the roof of my mouth. He remembered how I liked to be kissed—strong and hard and demanding. The give and take between us was as hot as it was back then, and now, God now I was starved for him on an entirely different level.

He held me to him, the touch on my hips so gentle compared to the way he dominated my mouth. It was the perfect contrast, and the fact that he wanted me with this kind of intensity set all my nerves on fire.

"Warren," I said, sighing into his mouth. "Please."

He stopped kissing me in an instant, holding my face in his hands. His chest heaved against mine, his breathing as ragged as my own.

I furrowed my brow.

"Don't stop," I nearly snapped. "*Touch* me?" I meant to demand it, but it came out a question.

A smirk shaped those glorious lips, and he claimed my mouth again before I could breathe. He held the back of my neck with one hand, and trailed the other down my arm, over my hip. He teased the waist of my leggings, smoothing his hand over my belly before slipping his hand beneath the band.

"Ohmhgod!" I moaned into his mouth when his hand touched my aching center. It'd been so damn long, and with Warren's touch, every single inch of me clenched with *need*.

"Fuck," he hissed against my lips. "You're already so wet for me, woman." He groaned. "God, I've missed *this*." He emphasized the word by sliding a finger between my wetness, stroking me gently.

"More," I demanded.

Gone was my fear.

My reasons for not doing this for so long.

Now all I was, all that I possessed...was *want*.

And the only thing I wanted was Warren Kinley.

He sucked my tongue into his mouth, silencing my plea as he slid one finger inside me, then two. I whimpered again from his entry, from the way he circled his thumb around my clit.

Teasing.

Torturing.

My fast and furious Shark that liked the slow burn in the bedroom.

Hot damn, the man knew my body better than I did.

Swirling tension mounted and coiled low in my belly, the spark already there, an entire month of sleeping a hallway apart making me ready to combust in an instant.

He rolled his fingers, pumping and stroking as he made love to me with his hand. I clenched hard around him, nipping at his lip as I moaned.

"You want this?" he growled the question. "Tell me you need this, Nine."

"God, Warren. Yes," I said, breathless, arching into his hand.

A puppet to her master.

"Say it." He held me in trembling anticipation, right on the cusp of shattering.

"I need this," I breathed. "Fuck me...I need *you*."

"There she is," he said, a mischievous smile on those damn kissable lips. He circled my clit one more time before pressing down while slanting his mouth over mine.

The combined pressure, kiss, and his fingers inside me sent me flying. Sparks shot up my spine, warm tingles exploding over my skin. The deepest breath shot from my lips, a wave of pure pleasure pulsing over my entire being.

Warren gently held me, kissing me softly, working me down as he slipped his fingers out of me.

He instantly sucked one into his mouth.

"Mmm," he moaned. "That's better than any brownie."

My heart raced at the sight, at the lust churning in those eyes.

I wanted more.

I needed more despite just having a serving.

"Warren," I said.

The timer beeped, jolting us both.

"Time to wrap them?" He asked, his breath still ragged.

"Fuck the brownies," I said as I pulled them out and turned off the stove. "I want you."

"Nine," he growled. "I told you I was strong, but don't play with me like that."

"I'm serious, Warren. Please. Fuck me," I said, almost too timid for the phrase.

His eyes flashed wide and hot and wanting. He pulled me to him, fingering my hair in one hand. "Is it safe?"

"Yes." I sighed, nodding. "Married people do it all the time."

"Are you sure? You want this? *Me*?"

I hated how unsure he sounded, how scared.

"Yes," I said. "Warren, I haven't wanted anyone else *since* you."

He smirked, flicking his tongue over my lips.

I gripped his shoulders, clawing into the muscles, desperate to wrap my legs around him. The baby-belly wouldn't allow for that. I groaned, needing him inside me so much I couldn't think straight.

"Trust me?" He asked between my greedy kiss.

"Yes," I moaned against his lips.

He spun me around, drawing my back flush against his chest. He smoothed a hand over my breasts that were heavy and tight, aching for his touch. His other hand glided over my belly before diving lower. He hooked his fingers in the band of my leggings and tugged them down.

My heart raced, thundering against my chest with pure need.

He ran his hand down my spine, gently folding me, my elbows on the counter.

"Fuck, yes," I said as he slid my panties down.

A shiver rolled through his body, like my submission, my trust, turned him on.

A light tap on my bare ass sent a jolt of pleasure straight through my center. "I fucking love that dirty mouth of yours," he growled. I heard the beautiful sound of a zipper before I felt him hot, hard, and bare behind me.

"Ohmygod," I moaned when he teased my entrance with his tip. He'd reduced me to short, repetitive phrases.

Reduced me to pure sensation.

Nothing but heat and ache and sparks and need.

"I've wanted to get back inside you since the second I left." His voice was primal, closer to the beast I knew, the gravely tone making me tremble with want.

He smoothed one hand over my hip, the other over my back until he tangled his fingers in my hair. He tugged gently, and I craned my head around to catch his gaze.

The man was glorious.

Towering behind me, I was completely at his mercy.

He could fuck me hard and rough or gentle and slow.

He would be completely in control.

The realization tightened my insides, a string that connected us going absolutely taut.

His hand on my hip moved, stroking the lines of my belly. "You're mine," he growled, and though his touch was gentle, his words were demanding.

"Yes," I said, pushing back against where he tortured me.

Another rumble came from his chest.

"Say it," he demanded.

"I'm yours," I moaned as he slid into me an inch more. "Fuck, Warren. I'm yours. We're yours."

I was orbiting, totally on another planet with the way my body soared.

Each movement was a lit match.

Warren owned every sensation pulsing in my body, in my soul, and I was completely, utterly, *his*.

"Yours," I said again, sighing.

"Fuck, woman," he said and plunged inside me.

His full, hard length filled me so much I moaned.

Good God, I'd forgotten how big he was. How wonderful he felt inside me. How he seemed built for me specifically. Every single inch of him working to make me a weak, weeping, sighing, moaning, *thing*.

"Yes," I said. "Oh, fucking hell, *yes*."

"Nine," he growled, running his hands over me until he gripped my hips. He controlled the pace, rocking into me slow but hard and oh-so-good. "You're fucking perfect," he breathed, pairing each word with a pump.

Every time he thrust, the head of his cock hit that perfect spot deep inside me, the one that made my eyes roll back in my head, and turned my muscles into a quivering mess. I clenched around him, unable to hold back another wave of pleasure as he held me on the cusp.

"Damn, woman," he said, increasing his pace as I gripped him harder with my thighs.

"Yes," I said. I didn't know any other words. I was simply...*feeling*. "Warren," I demanded.

He reached around, stroking my clit with the sweetest pressure.

"Come with me," I demanded again.

"God damn," he hissed as I clamped down, tightening as I coiled and uncoiled.

He pressed back with the same pressure on my clit, and I shattered.

My entire body shook from the waves of pleasure that crashed over me, against me, inside me. His length hardened as he found his \ release, and he folded his chest over my back, molding himself to me as he growled. The vibrations from his breathing, the heat from his body, the way I still pulsed around him, it all wove together into this absolutely perfect moment.

And I *cried*.

Not bawled, but tears rolled down my cheeks without me being able to stop them.

Somehow, Warren had touched me on every level possible.

Gentle yet strong.

Hard yet caring.

The man had given me everything.

As he held me, lightly tracing the lines of my belly, of the shell where our baby grew...I understood something with perfect, terrifying clarity.

I fucking *loved* this man.

And now there was no going back.

CHAPTER 10

WARREN

I TURNED JEANNINE AROUND, wiping the tears from her cheeks with the pads of my thumbs.

"Are you hurt?" I asked though she looked anything but. She looked more vulnerable than I'd ever seen here, with a lusty-haze in her eyes that made me want to put that look there every day for...

"I'm in—" she stopped herself short, sucking in a deep breath. "I'm just so happy," she said.

A slow, easy grin shaped my lips as I kissed her wet cheeks. "I am too."

I'd never felt this happy before.

Never once had I been in love when I took a woman to bed, and now that I'd made love to Jeannine? I knew there was nothing better than feeling her, making her moan, tasting her. Loving her.

I parted my lips, knowing I needed to tell her. That she deserved to know how loved she was. But I quickly kissed her to stop the words from tumbling out. She'd only just now let me touch her.

If I told her the truth?

She may skip out.

My fierce independent woman who needed no man.

I wasn't about to risk it.

Not now.

Not when she'd let me *in*.

Carefully, I slid an arm underneath her knees.

"What are you doing?" she gasped, her arms flinging around my neck as I hefted her off the floor.

I cocked a brow at her. "You didn't think we were finished, did you?"

Heat blazed in her eyes. "Put me down! I'm a whale."

"What did I tell you about speaking badly about your body?" I sucked my teeth, shaking my head. "You'll pay for that."

Her eyes flashed wide as I stepped out of the pants still around my ankles, and walked naked to my bedroom...*hers*.

Was it ours now?

Give her time.

Don't push too hard too fast.

Well, not in the emotional sense anyway.

I laid her gently on the bed, trailing my fingers down her sides and sliding her leggings all the way off. I tossed them and her black lace panties behind me then tugged her shirt off.

A gasp ripped through me at the sight of her bare belly.

Mine.

She bit the corner of her bottom lip, nervousness flashing as she looked from it to me and back again.

"Beautiful," I said. "So, damn beautiful." I glanced up at her as I kneeled before her on the bed, my hands reaching toward her tummy.

She nodded again.

I knew I'd just been inside her, making her shake with pleasure, but I always wanted it to be her choice.

Where and when I touched her.

I never wanted to assume or take—despite the primal caveman roaring inside me to lay claim to every inch of this woman.

Mine.

Timidly, I grazed my fingers over her round stomach, sighing at the contact.

My baby.

I traced the line of her belly.

My woman.

I slid my hands around her curves.

My life.

I pressed my lips against her bare skin, feeling our child move under my touch.

My world.

A tight, firm tug yanked from my chest, grounding me in the present like nothing else ever had.

I love you.

A silent declaration to our baby, and to her.

Soon.

I would tell her soon.

But for now...I was all about showing.

I planted kisses to her tummy, moving lower, lower.

She arched her hips into my touch, a sweet sigh escaping her lips.

Slowly, I held her hips and traced my tongue over her clit.

"Oh!" She gasped.

I smirked, so fucking ready to worship this woman until she was a puddle sprawled on my bed.

I hummed against her warmth, lapping the combined

flavors of us, licking the length of her seam, relishing how her thighs trembled against my cheeks.

"Warren," she whispered, arching into my mouth. "Fucking hell."

Her warmth and that damn dirty mouth of hers went straight to my dick. It begged me to sink into her, hard and fast and furious. Claim her so well she'd never want to leave, but I simply growled against her and kept on devouring.

Slipping two fingers inside her, I licked and pumped until she was gasping and clenching. A full body shudder and a burst of flavor had me aching for her so much it almost hurt—despite coming minutes ago.

Fuck, this woman was everything.

But nothing could've stopped me from watching her shatter.

Mine.

After her breathing slowed, she tugged on my shoulders, urging me upward. "I need you inside me. Now," she demanded.

I chuckled, holding myself above her. "Greedy woman."

"You said to tell you what I want."

That's right. I had.

And she finally let me in.

"I'm at your service, Nine." I teased her entrance with the tip of my dick, her slickness sliding all over the head.

I clenched my jaw against a growl.

Glancing down, my abdomen brushing over her belly, I paused.

"What is it?" She panted.

"I don't want to crush the baby."

"You won't," she said. "I promise."

I laughed again at the need in her voice and grabbed a

couple pillows from the other side of the bed. "Lift that sweet ass of yours, Nine."

She instantly complied, and I slid the pillows underneath her, creating an arched angle that would let me slip inside without my weight touching her belly.

"You didn't have to—"

I slid all the way inside her, cutting her words short.

"Oh. *Oh!*" She moaned as I pulled out and sank back in, the angle allowing me to get so, so damn deep.

I took it slow, allowing her to re-adjust to my size, her walls hugging me in the tightest, most delicious way. My hands roamed freely, over her tummy, kneading her breasts, rolling her nipples between my fingers until they were pert. All while I tortured us both with agonizing pumps, drawing out the sensations until we were both in the most blissful agony.

"Warren, please," she said. "I don't think I can take any more."

I grinned at the lust in her voice, the haze of pleasure in her breath.

I locked gazes with her, holding us both at the edge of release, savoring the pulse of her body around mine.

The way we fit perfectly.

The way she felt like mine in a way no one else ever had.

"I'm yours," I said, wanting her to know I was just as completely wrapped up in her. "You know that, right?" I asked, another long, smooth stroke where I pulled all the way out, eliciting a whimper from her.

"For how long?" the question was a whisper between our heavy breaths.

I paused at her entrance, my brow furrowed.

Does she think I have an expiration date?

"For as long as you'll have me," I said, knowing I would always respect her choices. That *she* would have to choose me and not the other way around.

I was already a goner when it came to her.

I slammed into her, strong and slow, hitting that spot that made her tremble and weep around my dick. She gasped through her orgasm, digging her nails into my shoulders, her head thrown back, her eyes closed.

Watching her come made my release follow seconds later, and I held her as she shook, as we both came back to earth.

Slowly, I slid out of her, hurrying to grab a cloth and clean us both up before laying in the bed next to her. She instantly pressed her bare back into my chest, wrapping my arm around her. The position of that perfect ass threatened to have me start all over again. But her breathing had evened, and her muscles relaxed within my embrace.

For how long?

The question echoed in my mind as I listened to her sleep.

I'd wanted to tell her forever.

And I wasn't sure how long I could wait until I officially asked her to be *mine*.

"Whoa," Jeannine said, her eyes wide as she surveyed the coffee table in my entertainment room.

"It's the last item on the list," I said, motioning to the various candies, popcorn, and ice cream spread on the table.

"What? Binging junk food?" she laughed.

"No," I said. "Netflix and chill."

"Oh," she said, nodding. "I can't believe it's the last one."

I couldn't either.

A month and a half had passed since Jeannine had let me in, and though I still hadn't told her I loved her, I was getting closer every day. Each time she gave me a look inside, past her walls, I felt I might be able to tell her without it terrifying her.

But, I'd been enjoying each and every day—loving her, sleeping with her, exploring her, discovering her.

We were insatiable for each other, sometimes going days without leaving the house or putting on clothes.

It was perfect.

I tilted my head, watching as she grabbed her left side as she sank onto the couch, her brow furrowed.

"Feeling okay?" I asked, sinking beside her.

"Hmm?" she glanced at me. "Oh, yeah, we're fine," she said, glancing down. "Feeling a little crowded but okay."

"Then what is this about?" I smoothed the crease between her brow.

She wetted her lips, the struggle in her eyes easily readable. The woman wasn't used to having someone there to help with whatever she chewed on. She would get used to it though if I had anything to say about it.

"Thinking about the investor banquet," she said. "It'll be a few weeks after this one comes," she said, pointing to her belly. "And I'm just..." she sighed.

"What is it?"

"Opening a fourth location—in the pub-style building I've been telling you about—has been a dream of mine since *Nine's* became a hit. The owner has fought me for years but —like I mentioned before—is a Sharks fan and is finally willing to sell to me as long as I have a Shark at the banquet. I'm ready to make the building my own, with a little help, if I can a Shark to show up..." she flicked her gaze to me. "And get my investors to say yes."

"And?"

"Now I'm wondering if it'll put too much on me. Split me between too many restaurants and the baby."

"You won't be split, Nine," I said, shifting to face her. "You can give yourself wholly to both."

"Can I?" She pressed her lips together. "I know I don't speak about it much, but my mother...she was never there for me. She blamed me for my father leaving when I was a baby. Took it out on me. Constantly told me how much she resented me because she had to give up her dreams to raise me."

I flinched, grinding my teeth.

"And," she continued. "By the time I was capable, I left. I *ran* to Paige's and never looked back. I've never needed anyone since, and I've never had a second of regret for not even saying goodbye to her. My own *mother*."

She smoothed her hands over her belly, and I placed mine on top of hers.

"You are nothing like her. You could never be. Nine," I said, tipping her chin so she had to look at me. "You are already an amazing mother. The way you've taken care of you both throughout this, for without help for so long..." I raised my hands when her lips parted. "I know you didn't need help. But, you're incredible, and I'm beyond proud that you've let me be here for you throughout these past months."

"I'm glad too," she said, timid, like she was afraid of admitting it.

"You don't have to give up your dreams. You are the

strongest, fiercest, and most loving woman I've ever met. You will rock both positions—mom and Michelin star chef. I have no doubts."

She smiled at me. "Thank you."

"That's what I'm here for."

"That and junk food."

"Yes," I said, chuckling. "Now, are all the details for the banquet good to go?" I asked, wanting to be sure she'd talked everything out that she needed. The movie night wasn't important. She was.

"Yes," she said, nodding. "Everything is set. Rafael has been amazing. He'll be blown away when I announce him as head chef once the investors and the owner give me the go-ahead." She flinched a little, grabbing her stomach, but pressed on. "Bailey has already agreed to watch the baby for the night of the event. There is really only one thing I need..."

I raised my brows. "What is it?"

She bit the corner of her lip, drawing her eyes away from mine. "A Shark."

I snorted. "You're joking."

"Yeah, I know." She shrugged. "I can ask Gage or Rory. But the owner has singled you out as his favorite. I think meeting you will help him sign the deed over to me. And it would be nice to have you there. But it's fine...I don't want to take advantage of your position. And I know we've never discussed anything beyond the list and the baby being born—"

"Stop," I cut her off, once again forcing her to look at me. "How can you think that? I'm *here*, Nine. It's not because of a fucking list." I smoothed my hand over her tummy. "And it's not because of this miracle either." She arched a brow at me. "Well, it's not *only* because of baby-ball," I amended. "I'm here for *you*. If you asked me to get you the fucking moon I'd find a way. Can't you tell that by now?"

"Warren...I..."

"No," I said when she struggled to continue. "I get that you have done everything solo your whole life. I know you don't need me, and I'm not trying to force anything." I sighed, hating that I was terrified to tell her I loved her. Terrified she'd realize I wasn't good enough for her, not by a long shot. That she'd say she could never love someone like me. "I'm just saying that...I'm here. For whatever you need. Whenever you need it. And if you'll let me, I want to keep being here, for as long as you'll have me."

A brilliant smile shaped her lips, and she intertwined our fingers. "Warren, I'm so in l—"

A gasp cut off her words, and she squeezed my hand so hard it *hurt*.

"Nine?" Panic clawed up my throat as I surveyed her. Her eyes clenched shut, her brow drawn together, a hiss between her clenched teeth. "Jeannine?"

She snapped her eyes open, gasping as she practically jumped off the couch. I followed her like a chain connected us.

"I think," she said between puffs of breath. She glanced from the couch to her leggings to me. "I think my water just broke."

My eyes widened, and the world slowed to a screeching halt.

Every thump of my heart shook my soul.

"Warren?"

Her voice cracked everything back to a normal pace, and I sprinted into action.

"Where is the bag?" I asked, scooping her off her feet.

"I can walk," she said, but I was already rushing through the house, her cradled to my chest.

"You can waddle, and we've got to go!" I said. "Where is the bag?"

She laughed.

The woman actually *laughed*.

"It's under the drop station by the door."

"Fuck, you're brilliant." I hurried to the entryway, grabbing the bag and rushing to my SUV. I settled her gently into the passenger seat and then fell behind the wheel, nearly reversing without opening the damn garage.

"Breathe," Jeannine said as I finally managed to make it on the road.

"Shouldn't I be telling you that?"

"Yes. Yes, you should." She cringed, gripping the door handle so hard her knuckles were white. "Fuck me, this *hurts*."

I pushed the gas, but kept it within the safety zones. We made it to our hospital in record time, and I was out and around to her side of the car before she could reach to open the door.

"You're not going to carry me inside, are you?" She teased.

"Can I?" I asked, not wanting to steal her independence but desperately not wanting her to walk through her contractions.

"Fine," she said, flashing me a pained smile while she gripped her back.

I scooped her up again, storming inside the hospital with my heart roaring.

After a quick conversation with the receptionist at labor and delivery, we made it into our room. A flurry of nurses came in and checked Jeannine after they'd had her change into a gown. I paced the room, giving them space while they hooked her up to what looked like way too many machines. Wrapping leads around her belly and placing an IV in her left hand.

"The Shark winces at needles?" Jeanine teased through her tight breaths as the nurses left with promises to be back in a little while as her dilation increased.

I sank into the chair at her bedside. "I'm not overly fond of them." I reached for her hand. "What can I do?"

"You being here," she said. "Is everything. Thank you."

I planted a gentle kiss on her palm. "Thank you for *giving* me everything."

She hissed, her grip on my hand tightening to the nth degree. I glanced at the machine next to her bed, noting the oncoming contraction. "It's a big one," I warned her.

"Great thanks," she snapped and clenched down on my hand even harder.

Fuck, the woman was stronger than I knew.

"Breathe," I said. "It's coming to an end. You're doing so amazing." She'd only groaned, not screamed like I'd seen in all the movies.

Her grip loosened as the machine showed me the contraction was ebbing, and I let out a breath as she relaxed too.

"Damn," she said. "That is horrendous."

"You're incredible," I said, smoothing back some of her hair. Her forehead was dotted with sweat as she blew out a breath.

"I feel like a car is continuously running over my hips."

I cringed. "You're officially stronger than all the Sharks put together."

"Oh, stop," she said, but another contraction came, and she went back to groaning.

I felt fucking powerless, watching the pain ripple through her. Nothing more I could do but talk her through it and let her crush my hand.

I'd never be as strong as her.

Never.

"Drugs!" She said after the umpteenth contraction. The nurse had just returned after an hour to check her progress. She flipped up Jeannine's gown, and her eyes widened. "Please," Jeannine said. "I'll take the drugs now."

The nurse shook her head. "Sorry," she said. "You've fast-tracked. You're at a ten. There is no time."

Jeannine whimpered.

"Isn't there something we can give her?" I snapped, never letting go of her hand. "Something to help? Are you sure she's at a ten? It's only been an hour!"

The nurse shot me a look that screamed *are you fucking kidding me?*

I swallowed hard, flashing her an apologetic look.

She nodded and called the doctor.

Turning my focus to Jeannine, I smiled at her, gently stroking her forehead. "It's almost over. You're doing so amazing. And we're about to meet our baby."

"But it hurts!" She growled. "I feel like I'm being split open *while* on fire."

I flinched, my heart breaking because I couldn't take that pain from her. "No one is stronger than you," I said. "You've got this. And it will be over soon." I eyed the nurse, who nodded again as the doctor came inside.

"Okay," she said, sitting on a rolling stool in front of Jeannine's wide-open legs. "Looks like we only need a few good pushes. I can already see the head."

My heart stopped and raced and then sputtered from the confusion.

I held onto Jeannine as much for support as she was me.

"Can you do that for me, Jeannine?" The doctor asked.

Jeannine nodded.

"Okay, try to push and hold it for twenty seconds."

Another nod, and then she pushed.

My fierce, incredible woman *pushed*. A low groan rumbled from her chest, but she fucking rose to every challenge.

This one would not sway her.

"Perfect," the doctor said, encouraging her to do another one.

Jeannine did, and I felt myself tensing with her, wishing I could give her all my strength.

"Almost there, Jeannine." The doctor glanced up at her. "One more good one and we should be done."

"Okay, okay." She breathed through her words and then clenched her eyes shut.

The longest twenty seconds of my life.

Every fear and worry shot through my mind like knives of ice as I heard nothing but silence fill the room.

Then...

A tiny, little wail of a cry.

The breath rushed from my lungs.

The nurse helped Jeannine pull the top of her gown down, and the doctor rushed to place a small, dripping with goop, red ball of a baby against her bare chest. My jaw was unhinged as I watched the exchange. Watched as Jeannine let go of my hand to cradle our baby against her, tears streaming down her eyes.

"Hi baby," she said. "It's okay," she cooed. "It's okay."

The nurse smiled at me as she shuffled around the pair, taking measurements, sucking gunk out of the baby's nose, and handing me a pair of scissors to cut the cord. Every motion flew by in a haze as I could barely take my eyes off...

My daughter.

"We have a daughter." My eyes coated with unshed tears.

"We do," Jeannine said, smiling up at me.

She was so beautiful.

Both of them.

In the instant that the baby stopped wailing and looked at me, I *knew*.

I was no longer tethered to this world by my own accord.

A tiny, eight-pound little girl owned my soul with *one* look.

And *she* became the center of my universe.

CHAPTER 11

JEANINE

I LAID the warm bundle that was my daughter in the bassinet next to our bed. Three days old and she was already an amazing sleeper, only waking up to eat. I knew from Bailey—who had too many sleepless nights to count from Ethan—that it was a godsend.

I tiptoed out of the room, closing the soft cotton robe around my swollen breasts. Breastfeeding had come naturally, but I was still getting used to the soreness. The nurses assured me the pain would lessen after a few weeks.

"Everything go okay?" Warren asked from his position perched on the edge of the couch. He was sorting laundry in front of his seventy-inch tv, which was on mute. I couldn't believe how many burp rags and onesies and cloth diapers we'd gone through already, and it was only day three.

I smiled and sank on the couch beside him, only slightly flinching at the contact. I was healing perfectly and was certain by the end of the week I'd be back to normal. Or, as normal as I could be after pushing a baby through my vagina. I chuckled at that thought, shaking my head in my palms.

"What?" Warren asked, grinning as he folded another burp rag and placed it on his growing pile. "Something funny about a Shark folding baby clothes?"

I laughed harder at that, nodding. "Well, yes actually." I reeled it in. "But I...I just can't believe I'm a mom. It's still sinking in, you know?"

He reached over and smoothed his hand down my back. "I know, but you're so great at it."

I snorted. "So far. It's easy right now. All I have to do is be a cow on demand."

He laughed. "There is way more to it than that," he said, continuing to fold. "I wish you could see yourself through my eyes when you're with her." He shook his head, his eyes wide. "It's incredible."

"Me?" I gaped. "You!" I nudged his massive bicep, savoring the warmth from his body. "I never knew you had it in you."

"Me either," he admitted. "But I'm so glad. I'm just so damn happy, Nine."

A thrill went through my overly exhausted body, waking my brain up like a shot of adrenaline. I leaned closer to him, nuzzling the stubble across his jaw. He set another onesie down and shifted on the couch the wrap his arms around me.

I tilted my chin upward, grazing my lips over his. He gently swiped his tongue against mine, and I sighed between his lips. Between giving birth and feedings and adjusting to my new instincts of being a mother, we hadn't had much time for...*this*.

He fingered the strands of my hair, scraping his nails

gently against my scalp. I practically purred as I pressed closer to him, wanting to feel his strong, solid body on mine.

"Warren," I said, whispering between kisses that became more urgent. My heart raced, my tired body working overtime to keep up with the desire that sizzled my blood.

"Nine," he said, smiling as he pulled back slightly.

"I know, I know," I said, chiding myself. "I can't help it."

"Trust me, I can't either," he said. "How long do we have to wait again?"

"Six weeks."

"Ouch." He flinched but replaced the move with a comforting smile. "It's good though," he said. "You need to catch up on sleep anyway."

I chuckled. "I do feel like I've been hit by a bus."

He kissed me quickly before standing. He scooped me off the couch, cradling me to his chest. "How about I put you to bed," he said, walking us quietly toward our room. "Then I'll finish the laundry."

"You are the perfect man," I whispered against his neck, squeezing him tight.

He was near silent as he entered our room and gave the bassinet plenty of space as he walked around it. Laying me down, he tugged the covers over my body and kissed my forehead. "Sleep for the few hours you have before feeding time," he whispered, holding back a laugh.

Thank you, I mouthed the words, my eyelids already half closed.

He smiled at me before walking toward the door. He paused by the bassinet, his gaze lingering on our daughter. My heart stuttered at the way he looked at her, at the life we'd created together. The way he had pride and love and complete wonder in his eyes...it made my entire body feel complete.

He winked at me when he caught me looking at him, and I shut my heavy eyes as he softly closed the bedroom door behind him.

This was my new life.

One I'd never planned for, but one that seemed absolutely perfect for me.

The warm blanket of sleep wrapped around me, but it was only after listening to our baby's breathing for a steady five minutes before I gave into exhaustion.

CHAPTER 12

WARREN

"KATHERINE KINLEY," I said, sighing as I gently placed my forehead against my daughter's. "You. Are. Killing. Me."

Her little forehead had been in a permanent scowl as she'd wailed for the last hour. Nine had handed her to me twenty-minutes ago, in tears herself. I took my little girl, now three weeks old, and told Jeannine to go take a hot bubble bath.

With headphones.

I bounced Katherine against my chest, shushing as I reached for the bottle of breastmilk Nine had pumped earlier. Bringing it to her mouth, I tried to coax her into a little drink.

That brought about another shriek that made every muscle in my body tense up.

I loosed a long breath, returning the bottle to its original place on the kitchen counter.

"What do you want, baby girl?" I asked, my eyes grainy like I'd rolled them in sand. "We've walked all over the house. I'm bouncing. You don't want to eat." I spoke to her in a hushed, loving tone, never wanting my overwhelmed and animalistic default settings to show.

But I was *fucking* overwhelmed.

I'd never taken care of a plant before, let alone another human. And despite the click of instant love that happened when Katherine set her eyes on me...I didn't have a clue how to be a dad.

Nine...she was a natural mother, regardless of her doubts and worries that she was doing everything wrong. I reassured her she wasn't almost as much as I tried to get this baby to sleep.

But, despite not remembering my last solid four hours of sleep, or smelling like baby puke constantly, or having Nine snap at me for something I hadn't even done...I was happy.

Genuinely, terrified, stupid happy.

Another high-pitched wail shocked all my nerve-endings, and I started swaying back and forth.

"Mama really needs you to stop crying," I said. "She takes it all on herself. Thinks she's not giving you what you need." I blew a raspberry, trying literally anything to get her to listen. "And we both know that's not true. So, what is it? Tell me, baby girl and I'll give it to you."

Not even a pause in her crying.

Just like her mother, she was going to make me work for it.

Make me figure out what she needed without her telling me.

I blew out a sigh, completely at a loss.

"Well," I said, shaking my head. "I'll just keep on holding you. Keep on waiting until you tell me what you need."

So damn much like your mom.

We hadn't had much time to talk the past few weeks—

not about anything outside of cloth diapers, burp rags, daily poops, and feedings. I was working double time trying to stay on top of Nine, making sure she ate and slept and got some good alone time when she needed it. She was doing all the *hard* work. Up every few hours to feed Katherine, or pump so I could feed her.

Plus, she really was taking on every little thing Kat cried about like it was personal. Like she was lacking as a mother. I knew it had a ton to do with hormones—thanks to a frantic call I'd made to Bailey two weeks ago.

But also, I went out of my way to make sure she knew how amazing she was doing. All of this in addition to planning the final touches on the benefit she had coming up that was so important to her. I didn't know another woman on the planet who could handle all that she currently was and still have stars in her eyes every time she looked at her daughter.

"You're going to be just like your mother, aren't you?" I said, whispering directly into Katherine's ear so she could hear me over her wails. They quieted as she nestled her cheek against mine. I laughed and whispered again. "You're so strong and fierce and a spitfire, just like her. Won't give daddy an inch, will you?" Her cries stopped completely so I hurried on. "It's okay. I love that about her. Love that about you. Don't you ever let anyone tell you different, baby girl. You don't give anyone an inch. Especially dumbass boys." Her eyelids drooped, heavy and slow.

The idea that one day she'd have to deal with guys pawing at her...fuck, it was enough to drive me insane. Invest in guns and shovels and buy more property perfect for burying a body.

"It's official," I whispered and bounced my way to our bedroom. "You've already made daddy a little crazy." I smiled as her eyes closed completely. "I love you," I said, swaying for a few more minutes before I gently laid her in the bassinet in our room.

The three words had proven effortless to utter to her, but much harder to admit to her mother. Before I'd been terrified she'd bolt if I pushed too far too fast, but now...now she had so much on her plate I didn't want to add more thing to it.

Besides, she *had* to know.

I showed her every day.

Confident Katherine was fully asleep, I tiptoed out of the room, shutting the door gently behind me.

Jeannine was in the kitchen, her soft black cotton robe wrapped around her, the ends of her long blond hair still wet from her bath. She opened and closed cabinets, a little louder than I'd like despite the bedroom being a good ways away.

"Shh," I said, more teasing than demanding. "I just got her to sleep."

"Good for you," she snapped, still rummaging.

I swallowed hard, my brow furrowing.

"Did you not enjoy your bath?"

She huffed, shutting another cabinet. "I did."

"Can I help you find something?"

"Sure," she said, finally turning to face me, her arms crossed over her chest. "I thought I asked you to pick up some oatmeal. It's good for my—"

"Milk production," I cut her off, nodding as I walked to the cabinet opposite her. I pulled the container down. "Steel cut. Just like you like." I sat it on the counter, raising my brows at her.

"Fucking hell you really are perfect," she practically hissed the words.

"You want to tell me why you're pissed at me?" I hadn't slept in days, which cut my filter-to-mouth ratio short.

She smacked her hands on her thighs, the sound of her bare skin making me wonder if she'd slipped on anything underneath the robe.

My mouth watered at the thought of her naked beneath it.

Fucking caveman.

"You just..." she sighed, almost a growl. "*You're* the one she wants. All the time. You're the one who gets her to stop crying. To sleep. To do anything. All I'm good for is milk!" She motioned to her swollen breasts, and I bit down on my bottom lip to hide my smile. "Oh, no," she snapped. "Don't you dare fucking laugh! It's not funny! I'm her mother. She's supposed to love me too. Instead, she seems to only cry when I have her." She sucked in a sharp breath. "She hates me. Just like I hated my mother."

I cocked a brow at her, narrowing my gaze as I stalked toward her. She backed up until her ass hit the edge of the counter, and I caged her in with an arm on either side of her.

"She cried ninety percent of the time I held her just now," I said, my voice low, primal. "It's a fucking coin toss on who will be the one to hush her, to relax her enough to sleep. It has nothing to do with *you* or *me*." I breathed her in, loving the way my body wash smelled on her skin. "But," I continued. "If you need to take it out on me, then go ahead. I can take it. But don't *you* dare take it out on yourself. Because you're the best fucking mom I've ever seen, and I have a hell of a good one. So I'm an expert."

Her palms flew over her face. "Oh my god, Warren," she said through her fingers. "I'm losing my fucking mind. I'm so sorry."

I peeled her hands away, catching her gaze. "Oh, come on," I said. "We both know you've always been a little crazy."

Her eyes widened, and she smacked my chest, but a laugh ripped free from her mouth.

One of the sweetest sounds in the world.

I captured her hand against my chest, stroking the lines of her palm and down her wrist. Stepping so close there wasn't a breath of space between us. "Better?" I asked, looking down at her, our bodies flush.

"Yes," she said on a sigh. "I'm sorry."

"Don't be," I said. "I'm a Shark, remember? I can handle you."

"How could I forget?" Something hot and needy flashed through her eyes, and she shifted against me, purposely rolling her hips against mine.

A warm shudder raked down my spine. I slid my hand down the side of her arm, over the side of her swollen breast, and lower, to the hem of her robe that stopped just beneath her ass. Slipping my fingers underneath it, I growled.

"God damn, Nine," I said, feeling the globe of her bare ass.

"What?" she teased. "I just got out of the bath."

"And you couldn't find a slip of fabric other than your robe?" I moved higher, massaging the small of her back.

She arched a brow at me. "I can go put something else on," she said, stepping away like I'd let her go anywhere.

I caged her in, using both hands to latch onto that perfect ass of hers, hefting her against me. A smooth smile shaped her lips, her hands braced on my shoulders. "Oh," she said, rocking her hips against me. "So, you do like me this way."

"Love you this way," I instantly corrected her, and it was the closest I'd come to actually telling her the truth.

Her eyes flashed wide before she slipped a calm, lusty mask over them. She reached up, grazing her lips over mine in a too light touch.

"Nine," I growled, slipping my tongue between her lips, needing to taste her. "How many more weeks?"

She parted for me, opening her mouth to let me all the way in, and I claimed it in the way she loved. Hard and dominate, my fingers in her hair, arching her head back for a deeper angle.

"I feel fine," she said, breathless against my kiss. She rocked against what was hard and ready in my pants. "I'm sure I'm fully healed."

Liquid fire rushed through my veins at the thought of sinking inside her warmth. Of hearing her sigh my name. Feeling her clench around me as I pushed her to the edge.

She hooked a bare leg around my hip, her robe hiking up so much I got a flash of what lay beneath.

"Fuck, Nine," I said, reclaiming her mouth, gently pressing into her as she continued to tease me over my cotton pajama pants. Just one barrier of fabric between us, her warmth soaking into it.

"Warren," she said, nipping at my bottom lip. Her eyes were molten blue and churning with need. "Please?"

"The doctor said—"

"I know my body better than a doctor who isn't even here." Her words were raspy, heavy, and lust filled. "I can feel you," she said, rubbing against me for emphasis. "It's torture."

I gripped her ass a bit more firmly, growling. "I don't want to hurt you."

"You won't," she said too quickly. "I promise."

"Nine," I said, the battle so damn hard.

We weren't supposed to.

I knew that.

Had listened intently when the nurses had told me why.

But for the life of me I couldn't remember the reasons. Couldn't think about anything outside of the woman in my arms. How much I loved her. How much I wanted to worship her until she was a limp mess in our bed.

"Fine," she said, reaching down between us. "Let me just feel you then." Her fingers slid between the slip in my pants, her eyes flying wide when she found nothing underneath.

I didn't get a chance to explain why I went commando in my house before she wrapped her hand around my rock hard dick and yanked it free. A breath and she'd parted, pressing my tip to her hot, wet center, coating it in her slickness. She arched her hips, sliding up and down and around my dick, her eyes fluttering shut from the contact.

I placed both my hands on either side of her on the counter, gripping it like it would keep me steady. I knew we couldn't make love...we *couldn't*...but god damn this woman was making it hard as hell to think straight.

"Mmmm," she moaned as she circled my tip around her clit. "Damn, I've missed this."

I growled, my grip on the countertop increasing. I locked my thighs, demanding all my muscles not to move when all I wanted was to sink inside her and pump.

She opened her eyes, locking with mine as she planted a slow kiss on my lips at the same time she slipped me inside her just an inch.

"Fuck," I hissed through clenched teeth. My body a statue other than my ragged breath.

She flicked her tongue in my mouth, still watching me as she sank another inch on top of me.

Another warm shudder ran the length of my body, my dick pulsing and aching, begging me to fucking *move*.

Thrust.

Pump.

"Warren," she gasped, rocking against me, slick and hot and so damn tight.

"Does it hurt?" I asked, growing harder the more I watched her use me to fuck herself. I wasn't sure there was a sexier sight on the planet.

"God, no," she said, sighing. "Warren, please."

I shook my head, the only movement I allowed myself. "I can't, Nine."

"Why?" she whimpered, stopping her movements.

I swallowed hard. "I refuse to hurt you," I said. "But keep going. I won't move. You do what feels right and feels good."

"That's not fair to you," she said, her tongue trailing the length of my bottom lip. "I want you. All of you."

"And I want to fuck you right here against the counter until you see stars," I growled. "But I refuse to do it one day sooner than they said." I claimed her mouth, kissing away whatever argument she was about to make. "Now," I said, tearing my lips off hers, our noses touching. "Why'd you stop?" I smirked.

She arched her brow, a challenge sparking in her eyes. "You like the torture?"

"I like watching you come."

She trembled against me, and slowly, agonizingly, started moving again. I sucked in a sharp breath, pressing my forehead to hers as she rocked against me.

"Warren," she sighed my name again, and I swore I was going to crack the countertop I gripped it so hard.

Mine.

This woman.

She stroked my cock, fisting and pumping it as she rubbed it against where she needed me most. Slipping me in and out, only the tip, enough times to make my knees feel like they would buckle.

"Oh, damn," she said, her head arching back as she upped the pace.

"Fuck," I hissed again, her hand working so fast, her center so wet and warm and clenching. "Nine," I growled, feeling that familiar tingle up my spine.

Fucking hell the woman was about to make me come from just her hands.

"Yes." She moved faster, pumping, and sucking my tongue into her mouth as she trembled around me. She moaned, long and hard, and I swallowed it with my kiss. My release flowing through me as fast and frantic as she shook against me. My entire body jolted with the power of it.

After we caught our breath, I let go of the counter, my knuckles barking from the blood that rushed back to them. Reaching for a towel, I gently cleaned up between us, my smooth, lazy strokes causing Jeannine to tremble all over again.

I smiled, shaking my head.

"What?" she asked.

"You," I said.

"What about me?"

"You're wicked. Making me break the rules," I teased.

"Technically we didn't break any rules."

I swiped my tongue over her lip. "You sure about that?"

"Absolutely," she said. "But if you want to, I'm ready."

I sucked my teeth. "Greedy woman." I smirked. "I *will*. In three weeks when we're clear."

Her shoulders dropped, but I tipped her chin up.

"And when that day comes?" I smirked. "I'm going to fuck you so hard and long you won't know any word outside of my name."

Chills coated her skin, and she shuddered against me.

"Warren," she said, her lips brushing mine. "I—"

A sharp wail cut off her words, and we both clenched our eyes shut for a moment.

"I've got her," I said, laughing. "You keep thinking about what I said. Feel free to touch yourself and go back for seconds."

I winked at her before heading toward our bedroom.

Toward the gift she'd given me, and thinking about the future I couldn't wait to experience.

CHAPTER 13

JEANNINE

"DUDE," Rory smacked Gage's chest as they stood at the table in my restaurant. "This is weird as shit."

Gage laughed, one hand squeezing Lettie's shoulder who bounced in front of him.

"What?" Warren asked. "Green is my color."

The guys laughed, eyeing the Shark-green Mobi that wrapped around Warren's sculpted chest, our baby between it and the fabric. I'd offered to wear it after we'd parked outside, but he'd insisted I needed a break.

It had been three long weeks of constant feeding or diaper changing or feeding again. I'd barely changed out of my robe and nursing bra the entire time because it seemed I was being used for food every hour or so.

I didn't mind, save for one mental break in the kitchen a couple of nights ago.

Thankfully, Warren sorted me out.

A warm chill raced across my skin at the memory.

Shaking it off, I sighed. There was something magical about the process of feeding her, about being so close to our baby, about providing for her. I'd never loved anything more in my entire life. It was like my heart had been entirely remade and placed outside my body into the little bundle that nestled now against Warren's chest.

I'd also never been more terrified.

Without Warren reassuring me all the time...I think I would've lost it.

I couldn't help it—I was scared of not being enough for her.

"Lucky for you Paige found one in the Shark's colors," Rory said, fist bumping Warren as he settled into a chair beside his boys.

"Thank you," Warren said, eyeing Paige across the table.

"You're so welcome," Paige said, wrapping me in a huge hug before I settled between her and Bailey.

"Not going to lie," I said, situating the baby bag beneath my chair. "This is a bit...weird."

"What?" Bailey asked, setting a handful of cheerios on Ethan's highchair tray that was scooted up to the restaurant table. "Katherine's first outing?"

I laughed. "Well, that," I said, "and the fact that I'm not in the kitchen with my chef jacket on."

Warren flicked his eyes up to me, taking them off our baby for the first time since he sat down. "You'll get back to it soon enough," he said. "Enjoy the time you have."

That was the truth.

Work wasn't going anywhere.

I'd cherish these few months home with our baby. Plus, I was damn lucky my sous chef was running things so smoothly, I could technically just sit back and watch it run if I wanted to.

"Getting any sleep?" Gage asked me from across the table after we'd ordered drinks.

"A little bit," I said and nodded to Warren. "He gets more than me."

"Five minutes more doesn't count." Warren chided. "Plus, I'd give anything to be able to get up with her more, but she only wants the boobs."

I laughed at that. "True."

"It won't always be like that," Gage said and smiled down at Lettie who was quietly coloring, then at Ethan—who looked exactly like his daddy—as he chomped away at those cheerios. Bailey reached over and squeezed Gage's hand, and I couldn't help but smile at the way our table overflowed with love.

We had created our own family over the past couple of years, and I couldn't be happier with the people we'd chosen for our inner circle.

Paige handed a wiggling Daphne—all blond hair and green eyes—to Rory before she snapped a picture of Warren wearing our baby, and we all laughed.

"What?" She asked, slipping her cell back in her bag. "It's baby's first outing. Things like this must be documented."

Warren smoothed his fingers over Katherine's head that peaked out of the fabric, her eyes closed in a blissful daddy-wrap sleep. He was so at ease. Wore the dad-role so handsomely. My heart expanded another size, all at once so full I thought I might cry from happiness.

"Thanks for being here," he said before glancing at me. "We needed the outing. We've been figuring out how to navigate all of this as we go, right?" He chuckled.

"Absolutely," I said, grinning at him. Wasn't that what we'd been doing all along? Since the moment he found out about the baby? It'd been one big experiment. One big trial and error run, and we were just lucky as hell that it worked out the way it did.

I had a feeling the next eighteen-plus years would be like that.

A picture took shape in my mind with the thought— Warren and myself in an audience of parents watching kids walk across a stage to earn their diplomas. My eyes snapped to Warren, and my heart skipped a beat. I hadn't allowed myself to think past the baby being born. Hadn't really given the future as much thought as perhaps I should've.

But looking at him now, at how these past few months had been, I knew I didn't want to be with anyone else.

I wanted this.

I wanted him.

Our family. Together.

I loved him.

But I hadn't said it yet.

And neither had he.

Sure, we'd both said it to the baby...but we'd only been together a few months. Was it too soon? I sipped my ice water in an effort to calm my nerves. Everything had happened so fast with us, and I was terrified of making the wrong move and bursting the blissful bubble we'd come to live in. Plus, I hated to admit it, but I wasn't certain if he'd be the same Warren when the season started.

I swallowed my fears as we ordered lunch and lost myself in the chatter between old friends. There would be time to think about the future later. Time to discuss what our lives were going to look like now that our child had come into the world.

We had time.

For now, I simply was happy to be out of the house. To be among the family we'd chosen as our own. And to watch the man I loved hold our baby with such gentleness it made me swoon.

Three hours later, Warren had secured our baby into the car seat in his SUV, and we waved to our friends as they drove off. Warren wrapped me in his arms after gently shutting the door as to not wake up Katherine.

"That was fun," he said as I clung to his hard middle.

I nodded against his chest.

He shifted, forcing me to look up at him. "Everything all right?"

"Yes," I said, my heart so big it was in my throat. The words were ready to burst from me, but I was so, so terrified. I didn't want him to leave. Didn't want to spook him. Though, he'd watched me give birth so what harm could three little words do?

"She did good." Warren glanced behind me through the window, rubbing his hands up and down my back. "We're lucky," he said.

"Yeah, we really are," I agreed.

I tipped my chin upward, brushing my lips over his. Unable to say the words I was dying to.

Instead, I decided to kiss him for all I was worth. I clutched at the muscles in his back, pressing my body against his as if I could mold myself to him right there in the parking lot. I sucked his tongue into my mouth as he cradled my face, taking everything I could from him and giving it all back, too. My blood was on fire with his touch, and I ached for him. We had a few weeks left to wait, but damn it I didn't want to.

I wanted to feel him again.

All of him.

"Damn, Nine," he moaned into my mouth, and shivers

raced across my skin at the lust in his voice. I loved that just a kiss could get him as revved up as me.

"Warren," I sighed against his lips. "I—" The words were right there, but I swallowed them. I wouldn't ruin this with words.

Coward.

His kiss was fierce and strong and consuming, and I trembled within his arms.

He drew back, our chests heaving against each other. A smirk shaped his perfect lips. "You're impossible, woman," he said, laughing. "Come on." He opened the passenger side door for me. "Let's go home and take a cold shower."

I smiled. "Together?"

He hissed, his eyes sparking as if he could picture the two of us in the shower, my nipples pert from the icy water. A low growl rumbled from his chest as he shut my door and walked around the car to sink behind the steering wheel.

At the same time, we both turned in our seats to check on our baby, who slept soundly in her seat. We both spun back around as he started the car.

"Thank you," he said, his voice almost a whisper as he navigated us toward home.

"For what?" I asked, tilting my head.

He shrugged, his eyes distant on the road. "Everything."

CHAPTER 14

WARREN

"YOU LOOK like one happy piece of shit," Rory said, fist-bumping me as we met outside of the small shopping center.

"Thanks, asshole," I said, laughing as I nodded to Gage.

"Kat still refusing to sleep?" Gage asked.

"Yeah," I said. "I don't know what it is. She slept perfect the first week of her life, and then a switch flipped."

"It'll get easier."

"So you keep telling me." I shrugged. This was my first solo outing since she was born, minus the dinner we'd all attended a few nights ago. I felt a little like I'd left an arm back home. "Thanks for meeting me."

"Anytime, man," Rory said. "You know that." I nodded as he clapped his hands together. "So," he continued. "What are we here for?" He eyed the area. "I don't see the beers."

I chuckled. "It's not technically a boy's day out kind of deal."

"What's up?" Gage asked, crossing his arms over his chest.

Something twisted in my gut, and I took a deep breath. "I want to find the perfect ring for Nine."

"Holy. Shit." Rory's jaw dropped.

Gage simply nodded, an approving smile on his face. "Finally ready to tell her, huh?"

"Yes," I said. "But I want her to know I mean it."

"A diamond can't hurt," Rory teased.

"I want them to be mine. Forever. I can't stand not knowing anymore," I said.

"I get that," Rory said.

"It makes sense," Gage added. "Anyone can tell you're madly in love with her. And Kat."

"Right," I said. "Except Nine. She doesn't see it. She's so damn hard on herself." I sighed. "I'm hoping she doesn't shoot me down."

Rory jerked my head in a lock with his arm. "I'll stock up on the tequila," he said, releasing me. "Just in case."

I huffed. "Again. Thanks, asshole."

We laughed as we made our way into the jewelry store. I knew Rory was just messing around with me, giving me hell for being the last one in our trio to get engaged.

I hoped.

I hated that I didn't have a clue what her answer would be.

With Gage, and even Rory, I think they *knew* Bailey and Paige loved them.

Knew they were going to say yes.

But Nine and me?

We'd done everything backward.

Fucked first.

Then baby.

Then love.

And now I hoped marriage.

Holy shit.

I never once in my life wanted to be married. Never thought one woman would ever be enough.

But Jeannine wasn't just enough—she was *everything.*

She matched me on every level—pushed and pulled and owned every second of every day. If I got to spend the rest of my life with her...well, I'd be one lucky son of a bitch.

"Can I help you?" I young male sales associate asked as we headed straight to the clear glass case glittering with engagement rings.

"We're looking for a ring," Rory said, leaning his elbows on the glass as he surveyed the rings. I settled next to him, Gage on my other side as we scanned the goods.

"Wonderful," the man said, his eyes darting over the three of us. He pointed between Rory and me. "Grooms?" he asked then pointed at Gage. "Best man?"

I pressed my lips together to contain my laugh.

Gage couldn't hold his back, but then he nodded. "Yup," he said, motioning to Rory. "He's the high-maintenance one," he said. "He needs a big rock to know he's loved."

Rory gaped at him. "Like there is a damn thing wrong with that?"

I snorted at the shocked look on the guy's face—like he was suddenly wondering if the three of us would start brawling right there in his place of business.

I waved them off.

"I'm proposing to my..." I tilted my head, never having put a label on Jeannine before.

"Girlfriend tonight," I finally finished.

"Oh," he said. "*Oh,*" he continued with a laugh.

"Still don't think I'm high-maintenance," Rory said, shrugging.

"Well, anything catching your eye?" The guy asked, smiling at Rory's feigned offense.

I glanced over the array of diamonds, some big and simple, some encrusted with smaller diamonds, and more. The case was stacked with rings, and yet I wasn't sure which one she would like.

"I don't know," I said.

"What kind of jewelry does she like?" he asked.

"I...I don't know," I said, racking my brain. She didn't wear much, which made me lean toward a simpler route.

"Um," the man said. "That's all right. Do you know if she prefers a certain cut?"

I swallowed hard, hating that I didn't know the answer. We hadn't spoken about these types of things.

Ever. We'd been so focused on the baby...

"Don't complicate it," Gage said, almost a snarl. He tapped my chest, forcing me to look at him. "Just check them out, and see which one you think would look best on her finger."

"Right," Rory added, cutting a glare at the salesman.

It wasn't the guy's fault. He had no way of knowing that I was lacking in certain knowledge when it came to Nine. Everything between us had been a fast, frantic frenzy.

Maybe I should've asked her.

Maybe I should've paid better attention.

Maybe I was an idiot about to get shot the fuck down.

"Trust me," Gage said, and I shook off the doubt creeping into my blood.

I nodded, slowly walking the line of the case. Clearing my head of all thoughts except the future I wanted to have with Jeannine.

Waking up to her in the morning, worshiping her at night.

Chasing her and Katherine around the house.

The guys and their families around our table for holidays.

Jeannine opening more restaurants.

Me winning more championships.

Until we both decided we'd reached our dreams enough and retired. Together.

"This one," I said, pointing to a simple yet elegant single stone diamond on a platinum band.

"You're sure?" The man asked, and all three of us snapped our heads to him. "Excellent choice," he said quickly. "I'll wrap it up for you."

"Thanks."

Gage clapped me on the back as the guy gathered the ring into a box and headed to the register. "Good job, man."

"You *do* have taste," Rory said, looking prouder of me than when I assisted him in scoring the winning shot against Ontario two years ago.

I rolled my eyes. "Right," I said. "Now I just have to figure out what to say."

"You'll figure it out," Gage said. "Just like you did today."

I nodded, handing the sales guy my card. He gave me a blue bag after I signed.

The guys followed me out of the store, each of us slipping on our shades as we noticed the paparazzi across the street.

"Fuck," I hissed, and Rory casually took the bag from my hand.

"Until you're ready to go public," he said, smirking. "Let them think I bought Paige another piece."

"Thanks, man."

"Of course," he said, then glanced around. "Now can we track down the beer?"

———

Beers turned into a three-hour pool and burger fest, and I hadn't realized how much I needed the escape until the guys were saying goodbye and I was heading home.

They helped distract me from myself, from over-thinking what I was about to do.

I gripped the steering wheel, terrified of letting go as I pulled into the garage.

Once I did, I'd ask Jeannine the most important question I'd ever asked anyone before in my life.

Breathe.

I sucked in a breath, and let go.

Walked into the house, the ring box tucked safely into my pocket.

"Nine?" I called through the house and was instantly met with the harshest *shush* I'd ever received.

Two seconds later Jeannine rounded the corner, skidding to a stop in the kitchen with her hands raised. "I just got her down," she snapped.

Oh fuck.

She had a *bad* day.

Her hair was in a wild knot on the top of her head, her shirt stained with what could only be Katherine-spit-up, and the creases in the corners of her eyes were etched in a permeant grimace.

"I'm sorry," I whispered, going to lean against the island. "You okay?" I asked even though I knew it was a dumb question.

"No, I'm so far from okay." Her tone was half-angry,

half-desperate, her blue eyes dulled to the point of exhaustion.

And it was that hint of desperation that made me realize...this was the first time I'd left her alone all day with the baby. No one here to help, she'd had to handle everything solo.

Fuck.

It didn't matter that was the way she normally preferred things.

I hadn't even called to see if she needed anything.

I'm a dick.

"Kat cried the entire day. Like, didn't even stop when she was eating. She cried around my nipple!"

"Is she pooping okay?" I asked, wishing I could find the solution.

Nine rolled her eyes at me. "Yes," she said like it was the dumbest question in the world. "Of course, I checked that. And she wasn't hungry. She wasn't tired. She didn't have a fever. She was just pissed off...*all* day."

And now *she* was the one who was pissed.

Perfect time to propose.

My internal voice had a real fucking funny sense of humor.

"And you were gone," she continued. "And left your pick-up game shit *everywhere*. I almost tripped while holding Kat."

I furrowed my brow. "It was just my bag—"

"You said you'd be gone an hour," she cut me off. "What happened? You couldn't call?"

I raised my hands, my mouth opening and closing a few times. "I went out with the guys for...we lost track of time."

"Yeah," she said, huffing. "Thanks for that."

"Hey," I snapped, unable to keep the adrenaline from

my veins. "I get you had a shit day. And I'm sorry I wasn't here for it. I'm here *now* so tell me how to help you."

Tears glittered in her eyes, but they weren't sad tears. They were shaped from anger and sleep deprivation and all things I couldn't even begin to understand. "You always need me to *tell* you what to do. Fuck, can't you just *do* it without me asking?"

I cocked a brow at her, feeling her words like a blow. "Not when I have no clue what you want."

"*Help*, Warren." She hissed. "I wanted help. Like four hours ago when she'd been on a three-hour cry-fest with no breaks."

I took a breath to calm the anger threatening to rise up my throat. "I said I was sorry. I'm here now, Nine. Why don't you go take a bath? Or go over to Bailey's. Do something for yourself. I'll take over for the rest of the night."

She rolled her eyes. "You don't get it, do you?"

"Clearly I don't."

"You weren't *here*. Because you were with your *Sharks*."

"What?" My head snapped back like she'd slapped me. "You love Rory and Gage."

"Yeah," she snorted. "And how much do you love the team, huh? So much that you don't want to be here, right?"

"What the absolute hell?"

"Admit it, Warren. Just do us both a favor and finally admit that we'll always come second." Now her eyes shifted from irrational anger to frigid fear.

"You can't believe that—"

"What am I supposed to believe?"

"That I've been here every second of every day since I found out you were carrying my child."

"And now that she's here? What are we?"

"Everything!" I couldn't contain my shout.

A wail ripped through the house, searing each of my nerve-endings.

"Oh, fucking perfect!" She yelled back. "Why'd you even bother coming home?"

I gaped at her, my chest feeling like she'd taken a fucking sledgehammer to it.

"Nine," I said, the air sucked from my lungs. "Tell me what to do to fix this." I knew she was over-tired, knew she'd been bottling something up for far too long and it was unleashed on me, but holy fucking hell I didn't know what to do.

"Leave," she hissed. "It's what you want to do. It's what you were always going to do."

I stumbled back like she'd punched me.

Where was this coming from?

She swiped at her tears before spinning on her bare feet, and rushed to our room. Katherine quieted after a few moments.

She'd kicked me out.

She didn't want me.

Want a life chained to a Shark.

One step back, then two, I made it to the garage, got in my SUV, and drove away.

Away from my home.

Away from my world.

Not having a fucking clue what had just happened, but feeling a hell of a lot like I'd just been part of a blast set to kill me.

CHAPTER 15

JEANNINE

THE PICTURE.

It was the *picture's* fault.

Sometimes I wished my cell didn't have internet.

Normally, it was a godsend while I fed Katherine. I could catch up on the news or read food blogs while she ate.

But earlier...I'd seen a picture of Warren and some random puck bunny, her hands all over his chest.

And something inside me *snapped*.

The loving energy that had buzzed in my soul clamped down, draining me more than the lack of sleep I'd had the past few weeks.

"What?" Paige and Bailey asked over the phone as I explained to them.

"Hold on," Bailey said. "Let me find the photo."

"Same," Paige said.

"Why does it matter?" I asked, rubbing my forehead while I held the phone to my ear. I'd called them in a panic after I'd gotten Katherine back down. After I came out of the bedroom and found the house empty.

He actually left.

I asked him to, but he actually *left.*

After a few seconds, I heard Paige sigh. "Oh, Nine," she said.

"Um," Bailey said.

"Right?" I sank into the kitchen nook's chair. "His first moment of freedom today and he *runs* back to his old ways." And despite being absolutely crushed, despite being horribly angry at myself for allowing myself to get hurt, I almost couldn't blame him.

"We never defined...us," I continued. Never had the big talk on what we meant to each other, but I swore I'd *known*. Felt it in my bones like truth. I'd been so wrong. "But I never expected him to do that. To go back to the playboy life without even giving me a heads up about it."

"No, Nine," Paige said. "You don't understand. He *didn't*."

"Agreed," Bailey said.

"How can you two say that? Look at the way she's touching him!"

"I'm coming over," Bailey said and hung up before I could argue.

"I have a meeting in an hour," Paige said. "But listen to me, okay? Please? I know you're exhausted and in such a vulnerable place right now. A situation you've never been in before, but he didn't do anything. I know for a fact."

"How?" Betraying hope snaked into my veins, warming me, calming me.

"One, because Rory told me exactly what they did today, and I know when he's lying." She grew quiet for a moment like she was paying attention to something on the other end of the line. "And two, that's Rory and Gage in the corner of the photo. Rory wore that shirt weeks ago after a pick-up game. I'm pretty sure he even mentioned the chick when he got home. Something about the bunnies coming out early this year or something. Wanted to warn me about it after all the trouble we had with Linda."

"Oh, holy hell," I said, my head sinking into my free hand. "He didn't rush out to his old life today?"

"No, Nine, he really didn't."

"What was he doing?"

"I can't tell you that. I can only tell you that he wasn't anywhere near a bunny, and I honestly don't think this picture proves anything more than the paparazzi drumming up gossip on a slow news day."

"Shit. Shit. Shit."

"It's okay," she said. "It happens to each of us. The first time you deal with this kind of b.s., it's tough. You didn't do anything wrong."

I went off on him.

Like mad-woman send me to the crazy house off on him.

I'd spewed every dark fear I'd ever had about loving him, right in his face. Accused him of wanting to leave us, just like I was terrified he'd always do.

Hockey first. Baby second. Me last.

I heard a car door shut outside, and for half a second I hoped it was him, but a knock on the door told me otherwise. "Bailey's here, Paige. I'll call you later." I sighed. "And thank you. Sorry for all the crazy."

"You're not crazy. And it will work out. I love you," she said.

"Love you, too," I said before hanging up.

I let Bailey inside, and she immediately hugged me before taking a seat across from me at the kitchen table.

"I'm such an idiot!" I snapped.

I needed to apologize to Warren. See if I could make him understand why I'd lost it.

"No, you're not," she said, setting her bag on the table. "This happens. This is what it's like when you're dating a Shark."

"I don't even know if we're technically dating," I said, pinching the bridge of my nose. "I'm so clueless about everything right now." Being a mom was the hardest thing I'd ever done, and with all the worry and strain of adjusting to my new role, I felt absolutely uncertain about everything else. I doubt I could even cook my signature dish properly right now if someone asked me to.

"Then I think it's time you go find out," she said. "You have bottles pumped?"

"Yes," I said. "Why?"

"Go find him."

"How?" I shook my head. "And where is Ethan?" I asked, noting the absence of the baby on her hip.

"Grammy has them both tonight."

"Okay," I said. "And why would Warren listen to me? I shouldn't have reacted that way. I was just...the day was so long, and Kat cried the whole time, and I don't think there could be one more drop of stress in my body right now, Bailey." I sighed. "I *blew* up."

"I know," she said, her eyes sympathetic. "And it's totally understandable. You're going through one of the biggest phases in your life right now. You're allowed mistakes."

"This one feels huge."

"He'll understand. Just go talk to him."

"Do you know where he went?"

"Gage headed to Phantom like two minutes before you called. Said Warren needed a drink." Bailey glanced at the video monitor that showed a sleeping Katherine in our bedroom. "He's likely blowing off the steam from the fight."

"Yeah," I said. "Or he's talking to the guys about the best way to get rid of me."

"Oh, stop it," Bailey said. "He wouldn't do that. It's just a fight."

"Is it?" I asked, shaking my head. "I lost my mind over nothing," I said. "It was like I wasn't even there. It was someone else. Some crazy, sleep and sex deprived woman. Not me."

"Isn't your time up?" She asked.

"Today." I pinched the bridge of my nose. "We were supposed to be able to try again today."

"See," she said, smiling. "There you go. Go get him, take him up to the balcony, and fuck his brains out. All will be well."

My eyes flew wide at her suggestion. "Who are you and what have you done with Bailey?"

She laughed. "Maybe your dirty-girl mission rubbed off on me."

I chuckled, using the lightness to ease the worry in my chest. "What if I blew it? What if I lost him?"

She gripped my shoulders. "You didn't. This is how life with a baby works. Craziness and passion and fights and making up. It'll be okay. Just go get him."

"Thank you," I said, walking toward the door. "Seriously. I don't know what I'd do without you and Paige."

"Same."

"There is pumped milk in the fridge and bottles in the top right cabinet," I said, my hand on the knob. "But she shouldn't wake up before I get back. We get back..." my voice trailed off as I wondered if he'd even want me to chase after him. Or if he needed his space.

"We'll be fine here. Take your time. Go."

"I love you," I said and wished it could be as easy to say the words to Warren.

"Love you, too. Go!"

I shut the door behind me and tried not to speed as I drove toward Phantom.

Fifteen minutes later and my hands were shaking as I entered the club.

The place had once been one of our favorite spots to hit, and while I knew I'd likely come here on girl's nights, it didn't hold the same allure it always had. The pulsing lights, the writhing bodies on the dancefloor, the vibrations of base from the music pounding in my chest, the drinks that never ended at the bar. It all seemed like a past life, a scene for someone with way more energy than I currently had.

And that realization made me smile.

Because I *was* happy.

Sure, I was upset that I'd lost my mind on Warren, but I was happy. We were happy. We had a new life to take care of, to nurture, to give ourselves wholly to, and it was a damn gift that we had this chance.

Why had I let fear keep me from telling him I loved him? I should've told him the minute I realized it. Should've let him know he owned my heart. My soul. He'd given me the most beautiful gift with our child, something I never knew I desperately needed until I had it. And I would always be grateful to him for that.

I moved through the crowded club, my eyes scanning for his sculpted body, that handsome face, those deep eyes. Where was he? Now that I was ready to pour my heart out to him, it was like I'd combust if I didn't do it soon.

Apologize first.

Right.

Apologize first *then* tell him I loved him.

God, I'd made a fool of myself. And I knew it wouldn't be the last, either. But I wanted him. I wanted a future with the three of us. He needed to know that, understand that I wasn't a crazy bitch that was using him.

I turned a corner, my heart full but my nerves frayed, and stopped dead in my tracks.

Warren.

He leaned against a thick black pillar that held up the balcony Bailey had mentioned earlier. A gorgeous brunette stood in front of him, her arm on one side of the pillar, a drink in her other hand. The same bunny from the picture. They looked *familiar* with each other. They spoke easily, freely, and there wasn't even a hint of him pushing her away.

As if he could *feel* my heart break, his eyes moved past the beautiful woman and widened when he caught my gaze.

I glanced down, only now realizing I'd shown up to Phantom in fucking yoga pants, a spit-up stained t-shirt, and my hair in a top-knot. I hadn't wanted to risk waking Katherine to change.

God, I looked like roadkill compared to the woman in the mini-skirt before him. A year ago, that could've been me...*was* me. And now?

I was a fucking moron for thinking he wanted this life. A life where he came home to a madwoman in shambles, completely coming apart at the seams from the task of trying to be the best mom in the world.

I backed up a few steps as he came toward me, calling my name.

I spun around and *ran* out of the club, gripping my chest like I could hold my heart together.

"Nine!" He called as I bolted toward my car parked across the street.

Tears streamed down my cheeks, and I cursed the hormones that had turned my normally steely self into a weeping woman.

"Jeannine!" He grabbed my elbow, finally catching up to me when I'd reached my car, and spun me around. "What are you doing here?"

"Me?" I snapped, my entire body trembling with adrenaline. "I came here to apologize to you. To explain why I lost my damn mind. What the hell are you doing, Warren?"

"Me and Gage were just having a drink."

I scoffed. "I didn't see Gage anywhere."

He growled. "That girl—"

"Don't," I cut him off, swiping at the tears underneath my eyes. "Spare me, Warren. I know it's been over a month since we've fucked. You obviously got tired of waiting for me to heal. And why not? I went off on you like a crazy chick, so might as well come here looking for a piece of easy."

"That's not how it is and you know it!"

I jerked out of his touch. "Do I?" I shook my head. "God, Warren it's only been a few months! How the hell am I supposed to know if we're *it*? Huh? If this was supposed to be more..."

"It was! It is!" His voice cracked. "Just let me explain—"

"No," I said, stopping him. A cold brick wall formed around my shattered heart, cursing me for giving it to him. "You know what, I'm done. I get it. You wanted to be part of Katherine's life and now you are. It was simply a bonus to make me fall in love with you, huh? That way I'd give you whatever you wanted."

He flinched. "Nine, don't. I love—"

"Save it." I snapped. "You wouldn't be here looking for *easy* if you did." I flung open my car door and sank inside. He stopped me from shutting it. "Don't worry," I said through my tears. "We'll be gone by the time you get back."

Warren went three shades of white and stumbled back like I'd punched him in the chest. I slammed the door shut, and sped out of the lot so fast I was surprised I didn't get a ticket.

The closer I got to home...to *Warren's* home, the more I crumbled. I'd been a fool to think I could have it all, but I guess it was better to know now.

Before anyone else could get hurt.

CHAPTER 16

WARREN

ALL THE AIR sucked from my lungs like I stood in the middle of a vacuum, not a fucking parking lot.

I gaped at the spot where Jeannine had just been, where she'd just *sped* away from me.

We'll be gone when you get back.

The words sliced through my chest like razorblades.

How had today gone past the point of fucked up?

Where had I gone wrong?

The ring box called to me from my pocket, begging me to rush home. Catch her before she could leave and show her what she meant to me.

But the other part of me? The one that was breaking inside...it froze me. The ice-cold fear thrumming through my veins only propelled me back into *Phantom* not away from it.

What if all this—Jeannine's anger and fear—was a way to cut ties between us? What if she finally realized that being with a Shark isn't what she wanted for herself, or Katherine.

Katherine.

My baby girl.

Fuck, I'd already let her down.

"Warren, man, what the hell was that?" Gage asked, glancing over my shoulder like he was looking for Nine.

"She wouldn't let me explain," I said, my tone almost too low to be heard over the pulsing music.

Fuck, why was I here?

She'd told me to leave. So I called Gage and he suggested a drink at our favorite spot. It seemed innocent enough, but then—

"There you are," Shay said, swishing back over to me. Just like she'd done a few minutes ago, spouting off score stats from last season like we were the oldest friends. I'd tried to be cordial, tried, once again, to shut her down nicely, but she hadn't listened. "You ran off so fast we didn't get a chance to talk about—"

"Stop," I cut her off, blocking the hand that reached for me again. "God damn it, I'm not some piece of meat you can put your hands on whenever you want."

Her eyes bulged, shock filtering across her face.

"I'm not interested," I said as clearly as I could. "I've tried to be nice, but you won't let up. Leave. Me. The fuck. Alone. I'm taken."

Her lips parted, her eyes shifting to anger. "You could've just said so. You don't have to be a dick about it." She rolled her eyes before clicking away on her heels, deeper into the club.

"Fuck," Gage said.

"I know," I said, rubbing my palms over my face. "I shouldn't have done that. It'll be all over the web tomorrow. But I don't give a shit, Gage. Nine *saw* me with her and thought I wanted my old life back. Thought that I could possibly choose that life over her."

"Shit."

"Exactly."

"Why are you still here? Go talk to her."

"She wouldn't let me explain. For the second time today." I sighed. "I think she's *trying* to end things." I shook my head. "She doesn't want this life."

"You don't have a clue what she wants because you won't talk to her about it."

"Who would want this? Bunnies and clubs and a constant stream of rumors you never know are true or not? Games and travel and—"

"Stop doing this to yourself, Warren." Gage cut me off. "I know you think you don't deserve her. Don't deserve the life that's been gift-wrapped for you with her and Katherine, but you do."

Numb.

It spread over me, silencing the roar in my chest, sliding a balm over the sting from the cut.

"Maybe she's better off this way."

"Maybe," Gage said. "But you won't know until you man up and talk to her. Make her listen to you." He clapped me on the shoulder. "This is a shit show, but we make it work. You've seen me, Rory. We make it work. And it is all worth it."

Something clicked in my brain, my mind finally catching up and restarting my body.

"I've got to go."

"Finally," he said. "I'll head home in case she went there, but I'll call Rory on the way to check there, too."

"Thanks, man!" I called over my shoulder as I raced out

of the club. It was agony waiting for the valet to bring my SUV around, but after six minutes I was finally behind the wheel.

I tried to call her as I drove, but her cell went straight to voicemail every single time.

"Damn it, Nine!" I growled, the numbness gone, replaced with a sizzling anger I usually kept on the ice.

Anger at myself, for not telling her I loved her sooner.

Anger at thinking I wasn't good enough for either of them.

Anger at Nine, for not giving me two seconds to explain.

And then, regret.

About my past, about something out of my control because I had no way of knowing how Jeannine would hit me like a falling star—all hot and sparking and fierce enough to shake up my world. My past is what made her believe I could actually step out on her, see a bunny on the side.

I thought I'd shown her all these months.

Thought I'd proved it to her.

I should've used words too.

Her car wasn't outside the house, but I was still the dumbass that hoped as I ran inside.

I knew the second I stepped foot into my entryway.

The silence was deafening.

No cries.

No gentle whir of the sound machine to help soothe Kat to sleep.

No gentle sucking of a breast or bottle.

No Nine.

The lack of life in the house hit me like a check to the boards.

I did this. I drove her away.

She'd really left.

And she'd taken Katherine with her.

I slammed my fist into the wall, my knuckles barking when it went clean through.

CHAPTER 17

JEANNINE

TWO MOVIES, two pints of Ben & Jerry's, and two feedings later, I sank onto Paige's couch, my eyes raw from crying. Katherine had finally conked out on my chest, snoring peacefully after doing her fair share of crying as I'd quickly packed us a bag and shuffled us over to Paige and Rory's house. Bailey following me.

Rory had come in the door an hour ago, bags of ice cream in hand. He wasn't at *Phantom* like I'd originally thought, but Gage *had* been there, as Bailey told me, but it didn't matter. Not anymore.

"Another round?" He asked, picking up the empty cartons.

I glanced up at him. "No, thank you," I said, my tone hushed so to not wake the sleeping baby on my chest.

He nodded and disappeared into the kitchen.

My cell vibrated on the coffee table before us, drawing me, Bailey, and Paige's gaze.

Warren.

I let it got to voicemail.

Again.

Every time he called I wanted to pick up, to hear him out, but then I'd see the image of that mini-skirt wench so close to him, so close to his body...and I'd cringe. The anger consumed any rational thought I may have had.

"Don't you *want* to answer?" Bailey asked.

"No."

"Nine," Paige said, sighing. "You know we love you. And support you no matter what, but..." she glanced at Bailey before continuing. "Crazy puck bunnies come with this Shark territory."

"I can attest to that," Rory said, returning to sit next to Paige in the armchair she perched on. "And, again," he said, rubbing his hand up and down Paige's back. "That bunny has been after Warren for months. He constantly shuts her down."

I huffed. "It didn't look like it."

It had looked like he was letting her *in*.

Rory grumbled and Paige elbowed his side.

"Thank you for vouching for him," I said, flashing Rory a sympathetic look. "But honestly, Rory. It's only been a few months." I shook my head. "He never wanted this." I glanced down at the bundle in my arms, at my heart that I held like it was the most precious thing in the world because it was. "He never signed on for this kind of relationship. He only wanted to be involved in the baby's life, and I think we got in too deep and he felt it and..." my breath caught as more tears threatened to stream from my eyes. I forced them down. I was done crying. "He wanted an out. He used the bunny as his exit ticket. And we're done." I sighed. "Who would want what comes with this crazy, stressful life when they could be a hockey star who can sleep with anyone he wants?"

"You seriously didn't fucking just ask me that, did you?"

Rory snapped, and Paige elbowed him again. "I'm sorry, Nine. You know I love you, but *fuck*. Gage and I both were in the same exact position as Warren. And look at us now."

"He's not you. He's not Gage. And it most certainly wasn't the exact same." I eyed him, then Katherine, and back again.

"Damn straight he isn't. He stepped up like a man the second he found out that baby was his. He didn't run from it. If anything, he embraced it a hell of a lot faster than I would've." He glanced down at Paige giving her an apologetic look. "It's true. I know I'd man up, but maybe not as fast as Warren did. He wanted this. He wanted you both."

"Maybe he did, in the beginning." I patted Katherine's bottom when she nuzzled against me. "But tonight...he went rushing back to his old life. And I can't even blame him for missing it. For wanting to be that free again." I could understand the urge to be free of responsibility again, despite not wanting to go back to that life myself. "And I bombarded his life with *this*. Turned it upside down with the news. And fuck me if I wanted him to choose me. Choose us." I shook my head. "But I won't force him. I would never want to force his hand like that. Trap him in something he doesn't want. So, he got his out." I sucked in a sharp breath, ignoring the pitying gazes of my friends. "And now I need to focus. I have a baby to raise and a banquet to host to get my fourth restaurant greenlit." The same function Warren had promised to be at. To help me seal the deal on the building...

An ache split down my chest at the realization that we were done. I'd gotten used to him being there for me, depended on him.

Loved him.

And now it was over.

Rory parted his lips, but Paige elbowed him again, and he blew out a breath, rising from the chair and disappearing to another wing of the house. I appreciated him trying to talk some sense into me about his best friend, but I couldn't hear it.

Not when I was in so much pain.

Not when all my fears had come to a head.

Not when I knew exactly what it felt like to *never* be chosen by a parent.

I held Katherine a little closer, thankful that I knew with absolute certainty that I'd never let her feel like a burden. Never let her doubt how loved she was.

I could be enough for her.

I *would* be enough for her.

And my broken heart would just have to heal another time.

CHAPTER 18

WARREN

CRACK!

My helmet smacked against the boards, Bentley's hit had the force of a Mack truck.

"So we're full force today, huh?" I snapped, shaking off the hit. "Good."

Bentley's eyes flashed wide beneath his helmet, but there was a challenging smirk there that said he *knew* I needed this. Gage must've filled him in before he dragged me out this morning.

After finding my home empty last night—both the loves of my life fleeing from my very existence—I hadn't wanted to move, let alone play a pick-up game.

But Gage and Rory showed up, packed my shit, and forced me into the rink.

Now I was glad they did.

The feel of my skates shredding the ice, the heat in my lungs from the level we played at—not easy like our usual pick-up games—the sweat dripping over my face, the burn in my muscles as I chased after the rookie to return the hit, it all focused me to the point where I could think clearly.

The physical exertion lifted the fog hovering over my brain, the ache splintering my heart. My first love soothing me like nothing else could, and making me realize how much more I loved Nine and Kat.

Smack!

I caught Bentley, slamming him into the boards so hard he lost his footing and crashed against the ice.

"Shit," Gage said, skating over to us, the game completely forgotten. Rory was right behind him.

I offered Bentley a hand up. "Gotcha, Rookie."

He took it, and righted himself, blinking the haze out of his eyes.

"Fuck," he hissed. "I'm glad we're on the same team." His breaths were fast. "I'd hate to play you when you're actually on point."

I raised my brows. "You think that was going easy on you?"

He tilted his head. "I *know* it was."

"Not bad, Rookie." I pursed my lips, nodding. "Not bad."

He rolled his eyes but didn't comment on the nickname I knew he hated, which was the only reason why I used it.

A moment of catching our breath and I realized...I stopped moving.

Stopped skating, playing.

Fuck, there it was, the storm cloud of thoughts rolling in to take over now that the distraction had paused.

"You didn't mention how Nine was," I said, eyeing Rory.

"She and Katherine are fine." I'd never seen him look so guilty.

"Don't," I said. "I'm glad she went to your place." I

glanced at Gage. "Would've been happy with her at yours, too. As long as she and Katherine are safe. Happy."

"She's not happy," Rory said, and I snapped my eyes to him. "Katherine is fine. Perfect, actually. But Nine? She's a fucking mess, dude. Went on and on last night about how she never wanted to trap you and pin you down when you like to be free. I tried to run interference, but Paige shut that shit down quick. She could tell Nine was in pain, and me speaking on your behalf only made it worse."

"Thanks, man. Sorry you were in that position." I sighed.

Trap me? Fuck, is that what she thought?

I bought a ring.

I wanted her to be *mine* forever.

"It's fine," he said. "Just wish I could've done something other than bring in a truckload of ice cream."

I laughed, the motion freeing up some of the tar that had caked around my lungs after last night. The weight lessening, the hope returning.

Just as quickly, it vanished.

What if she hadn't been talking about me? What if when she was talking about *me* wanting to be free and not trapped, she really meant herself. We'd both run wild before Katherine, and now that she was here...was Nine missing that? Craving it?

"What are you going to do?" Gage asked.

"I don't have a clue," I admitted.

Bentley cleared his throat, and I half expected him to motion over his shoulder to explain a quick exit from the heavy talk. But he didn't. He stood there, his stick in his hands, and there was something in his eyes...something like understanding and regret.

"I know I'm not up to speed on all the details," he said.

"But I've heard enough bits and pieces to paint a picture." He paused, gauging my reaction like he thought I'd tell him to fuck off. When I didn't, he continued. "I can tell you really love this chick," he said. "And that should be enough."

I raised my brows. "Enough for what?"

"For everything." He shrugged. "Circumstances shouldn't matter. Not when it comes to the woman you love. The chance to be with her every single day? Do you know how rare that is? How rare a situation each of you have?" he glanced over all three of us. "We all fuck up, make mistakes. But *you* haven't crossed the line where there is no coming back. Not even close. You still have a shot. And if you don't take it? You're a fucking idiot."

I jolted, shock coursing through me at the insight from the rookie.

"Damn," Rory said, gaping at me. "Rookie just went full blown Oprah on your ass."

Gage snorted.

I skated to within an inch of Bentley's space, our helmets almost touching. A tiny bit of fear sparked in his eyes before he flexed, holding his ground, chin held high. "Or," I said. "He's not just talking about *me*." I challenged, watching as a muscle in his jaw ticked.

"Yeah," he said. "Maybe I was an idiot. Maybe I wasn't. Maybe I just don't want every pick-up game to end up being an episode of *The View* anymore." He shrugged, but the cockiness didn't reach his eyes. There was real pain there. Experience. That was where this was coming from, and I actually felt bad for the kid.

"All right," I said, clapping my hand on his shoulder.

"All right, what?" He asked when I didn't continue.

"You are," I said, nodding. "You're all right, Rookie."

I skated backward to stand next to Rory and Gage, the three of us all in agreement. The kid had earned his place, me the last one to acknowledge it. "We'll have to celebrate your initiation later, Rookie," I said, glancing at Rory and Gage. "I've got a banquet to get ready for."

Gage fistbumped me, then Rory.

"Go get her, dude!" Rory called as I hurried off the ice.

Twenty minutes later I was back in my empty house, searching for my best suit.

Maybe she be pissed if I showed up.

Maybe she wouldn't listen to me.

But I had to *try*. Because this pain? This hole in the center of my chest where Nine and Katherine were missing? It was no way to live.

Rookie was right. I'd be a fucking idiot to let her slip through my fingers.

—

Nine's was packed for the private event, tons of press snapping photos of all the A-listers as they made their way inside. A few of which I assumed were her potential investors.

Luckily, the bouncer didn't stop me at the door. Instead, he held it open for me, giving me a thumbs up like he knew I needed the encouragement. More likely he was a fan, either way, I didn't question it.

I paused once inside, blown away by the transformation she'd done to the place for the event. Her usual setup of cozy tables and booths had been rearranged for a more open plan, allowing double occupancy. Tall, standing tables now scattered throughout the main room, waiters offering guests mini-versions of her specialties on cloth-covered trays. A champagne bar set in the far corner, along with another table lined with food. Music filtered lightly through the place, a background to everyone who chatted or laughed or ate.

Magic.

The woman was magic.

But I'd already known that.

I scanned the crowd as I weaved through the restaurant, my eyes grazing over suits and sparkly dresses, looking for one particular blonde I couldn't live without. After a few minutes, I was about to head to the kitchen when I heard her say *no*.

Snapping my head in the direction of her voice, I spotted her with her arms crossed, tucked into a corner by her actual bar. A tall man was in front of her, asking her something with his cell phone raised like a damn recorder.

One second I was standing among the happily buzzed crowd, the next minute I was *there*.

Jeannine's eyes flashed when she saw me over the guy's shoulder.

"We've heard rumors of who the father is," the guy was saying. "Everything from Hollywood's hottest bachelor to—"

"I told you I don't want to comment on that," she cut him off. "It's none of the press's business," she continued in a professional tone. "And it has nothing to do with tonight's events."

"Fair enough," he said. "Do you care to comment on the rumor you're tied to one of Seattle's Sharks?"

She bit her bottom lip, her eyes catching on mine. "No," she said. "My best friends are married to Sharks. That's all."

I felt the words like another blow, but I didn't flinch.

She was protecting me.

Didn't want to tie me to something she thought I didn't want.

Fuck, she really thinks she is trapping me.

I resisted the urge to roll my eyes.

My stubborn, fierce, woman.

"Excuse me," I said, tapping on the man's shoulder. He spun around, and instant recognition clicked in his eyes.

"Mr. Kinley," he said, excitement buzzing off of him. "Can I ask you about—"

"Not tonight," I cut him off. "It's a party," I continued, motioning behind us. "Go enjoy yourself." There was no room for argument in my tone. Lucky for him he picked up on it and made quick work of leaving us alone in the secluded corner.

"What are you doing here?" she asked, her voice almost a whisper.

"I told you I'd be here." I trailed my eyes up and down her body, smiling at the way the black dress hugged her curves and showed off her long legs.

"That was before," she said. "You didn't have to..."

"I *want* to be here, Nine," I said, my voice low, primal, as I stepped into her space. "Don't you get that?"

"I..." her breath caught as I came within an inch of her body.

"It doesn't matter if you try and push me away. It doesn't matter if you've made yourself believe that I don't want this. Want you. Believe this: I wanted you before Katherine. I haven't touched another woman since our first night together, that's how deep you're in me."

"All those months while you were gone..."

I shook my head. "No one else. Just. You. And I'm here. I'm right *here*."

"For how long?" she asked, the question echoing through my memory.

Bare skin and silk sheets and the smell of her all over me.

The memory was enough to make me growl.

"For as long as you'll have me," I said, and dropped to one knee.

Her lips popped into the shape of an O as I brought the ring box out and opened it before her.

"I love you, Nine," I said, gazing up at her, my heart fucking racing in my chest like I was speeding toward the goal in a shutout. "I don't know what I was doing before you," I said. "Before Katherine. But I want this life. Our life. You. Me. Her. Every day until the rest of forever. I don't want anyone or anything else." I smiled up at her. "Is that too much to ask?"

CHAPTER 19

JEANNINE

"I CHOOSE YOU," Warren's words rocketed through my entire body.

I gasped into my hand, wishing like hell my mouth would work but the words just weren't there.

"Nine?" He asked when I hadn't said anything.

I looked down at him, still on one knee, the ring before him.

Open, inviting, mine.

"Yes," I said, and I'd never been more sure of anything in my life. "Yes, I'll marry you."

He shot upward, his lips instantly connecting with mine. Electricity sparked across my skin, and my insides melted under his touch.

Home.

He was like coming home.

"I love you," he said against my mouth.

"I love you," I said, kissing him hard and long and probably way too intimate for the setting.

Applause erupted around us, reminding me exactly where we were and what I was doing. I drew back, but

Warren held me close as we turned to face the onlookers. Every guest I'd invited to my banquet was now smiling at us.

Mortified.

"I'm supposed to be hosting," I whispered to Warren, who laughed.

"All right, all right. Go. Work."

I intertwined our fingers. "Don't think I'm letting you go," I said, and tugged him around the room with me.

After mingling with everyone–including introducing Warren to the owner of the building of my dreams—and checking on the food twice, I was finally able to steal a moment alone with Warren. I pulled him into my office and locked the door behind us.

Warren cocked an eyebrow at me.

"I can't wait a second longer," I said.

"Oh, thank God." He pressed my back against the closed door.

"I'm so sorry," I said against his kiss. "I was so stupid and scared and—"

His tongue darted over mine, stopping my apology. "No," he said between kisses. "I was. An idiot. I—"

It was my turn to swallow his words. I sucked on his tongue, relishing the taste of him, the way he made me come alive with just as kiss.

"You really want this? Want us?" I asked, drawing back enough just to catch his eyes.

Nothing but sincerity and love shined back.

"Yes. You're all I want," he said, then his brow furrowed. "Are you sure you can handle being married to a Shark?" He asked. "You know what the territory comes with," he continued. "But I promise you, you and Katherine will always come first. No matter what."

I smiled, his words soothing every fear I ever had.

A smirk shaped my lips. "I can handle you."

A flash of a smile before he crushed his lips on mine. His hands gripped my ass as he hefted me upward, and I locked my ankles around his back, my dress hiking up so barely anything separated us. He was already gloriously hard, his perfect cock pressing against my lace panties.

It'd been too long.

Warren kissed my lips, my neck, and nipped at the spot behind my ear. Our touches were hungry, starved, and frantic. I clawed at his dress shirt, bunching up the fabric as I shamelessly ground against him.

"Now," I said, practically begging him. "We'll take our time at home."

"Home," he growled against my neck while he unzipped his pants. "When I get you there," he said, teasing the lace with his tip. "I'll lay you in our bed and worship your body for hours. So much you won't be able to see straight."

My eyes rolled back in my head, from his words and his touch.

"Yes," I said, unable to voice more. "Please."

He shoved the lace to the side and plunged inside me. I threw my head back, gasping at the contact, and the sweet, sharp way he filled me.

He was hot and hard and perfect.

"God damn," he growled, pumping as I gripped his shoulders. "I've missed you."

"I love you," I moaned, rocking my hips in rhythm with his thrusts.

"So damn much," he agreed, claiming my mouth, sucking on my bottom lip until I keened. "Say it, Nine."

"You first," I challenged, our eyes locking.

"You're mine." The statement was branding, like fire on my skin.

"I'm yours," I complied, trembling as he pushed me to the edge.

"And I'll always be yours," he said, kissing me so tenderly, such a contrast from the way he dominated me between my legs. "You've owned me since that first night."

"Fuck, Warren," I moaned, clenching around him.

"Yes," he said, pinching my ass enough for the bite of pain to push me full-on over the edge. "Love that mouth of yours."

I tightened my thighs around him, clenching harder until he threw his head back and hissed. He hardened inside me, his release only pressing mine farther, longer, more intense than I'd ever had before. I shook around him, quaked and trembled until I was sure my muscles were no longer solid.

We caught our breath, him holding me against the door like it was nothing. Those massive muscles of his not even flinching at what we'd just done.

"You're beautiful," he said, pushing the wild hair back from my face.

"You're not so bad yourself, Shark." He laughed, and I smiled against his lips as I bit his bottom lip. "Are you sure you're ready for a lifetime of this?" I asked, still in awe of what lay before us.

"I've never wanted anything more," he said, no hesitation or doubt or fear in his eyes.

I kissed him again, long and hard and full of my love. I let go of everything that had been holding me back before and submitted myself fully to the way this man loved me.

Loved us.

It was one hell of a place to be.

EPILOGUE

WARREN

KATHERINE'S EYELIDS DROOPED, over and over, as I whispered to her old Shark's stats until she finally drifted off. I laid her in the crib, taking a few precious seconds to watch her sleep, before quietly heading out.

Jeannine was in the living room, a bottle of champagne in one hand and two flutes in the other. The black silk robe she wore told me she had not a scrap of lace underneath, and my dick twitched at the sight.

The ring on her left finger? That made me full on hard and ready.

Mine.

It had been one month since I proposed to her that night—one month of baby chaos and bliss.

"What are we celebrating?" I asked, my eyes hooded as I greedily raked them over her luscious body. I stood my ground, wanting to draw out the moment, knowing she loved the torture as much as I did.

"I signed on the building today," she said, her smile warming my chest. "I'm now an owner four times over."

I took a few steps closer, allowing myself to be within touching distance but keeping my hands to myself.

"That's wonderful," I said, taking the flute she handed me. She quickly filled the glass, then hers, and we clinked them in a cheers. "Congratulations," I said before taking a sip.

"Thank you," she said, taking a drink of her own and chasing a few stray drops with her tongue. "I pumped enough earlier today that I'm allowing myself this one glass," she said. "And I can't believe there will be a fourth *Nine's*."

"I can," I said, setting the glass down on the coffee table. "You can do anything you set your mind to."

She arched a brow. "Are you buttering me up because the season starts tomorrow?"

My shoulders sank, the heat coursing through my blood fizzling. "I'm not, but..."

"But what?" She asked, stepping close enough that her silk covered breasts brushed my chest—the soft, supple contrast to my hard muscles made a hot shiver run down my spine.

"I'd be lying if I said I wasn't worried about it."

"You're the best winger the Sharks have," she said, trailing a finger over my chest. "You don't have to worry about the games."

I growled as she played with the hem of my cotton pants. "You know that's not what I meant."

The tease left her eyes as she reached up on her tip-toes and planted a soft kiss on my lips. "I know, Warren." She smiled. "I'm not worried, though."

"Honestly?" I asked, knowing me choosing my career over her and the baby had been one of her biggest fears when we first came together.

We'd gotten ten times better at communicating since I'd almost lost her and Katherine because of so many misunderstandings, but we hadn't actually been tested when it came to shuffling hockey and a family.

Tomorrow a new season would start, and while I knew Jeannine and Katherine would always be the most important things in my life, I didn't know if she fully believed that yet. Even if we were engaged.

"Honestly," she said, wrapping an arm around my neck, her body now flush with mine. "You think I'd accept this ring without believing you were giving yourself wholly to me?"

"I never want to lose you." I pressed my forehead against hers. "Or Katherine. If you asked me to quit, I would."

She drew back enough to catch my gaze. "I would *never* ask you to stop doing what you love," she said. "You wouldn't ask me to stop cooking, would you?"

I shook my head. "Never."

"Then we're the same."

"I'm so damn lucky," I said, trailing my nose along the line of her jaw.

"So am I," she said on a sigh, arching into me.

The motion drew a growl from my chest, and I claimed her mouth, hard and hungry.

"Nine," I said against her lips, my hands palming her bare ass underneath the robe. "You're killing me."

She laughed, a sweet sinful sound that promised more glorious torture. "I thought you'd like the new robe," she said. "Much better than the cotton one that was starting to wear *me*."

I chuckled, kissing the edge of her neck. "You look sexy in anything," I said.

"But this one," she said, reaching between us and freeing my dick from the split in my pajama pants. "*Feels better.*" She rubbed the tip against the rich silk covering her warm pussy, and I gripped her ass harder. "Right?"

"Mmmhmm," I said, unable to form a coherent response as she fisted me with lazy strokes. She moved and pressed me right where she wanted me, that damn warm silk creating this crazy combination that focused my awareness on one thing and one thing only.

Palming her ass, I hefted her against me. She locked her ankles around my back, her robe bunching around her hips, leaving her open and exposed to me.

Gently, I laid her back on the sectional, knowing we weren't going to make it to one of the guestrooms. I knelt between her legs, hooking my hands under her knees and dipping my head.

"Oh!" She jolted when I gave her seam one long, hot lap.

"You're delicious," I said, the vibrations from my words making her shudder. "And you're mine."

She moaned in response, arching into my mouth as I licked and sucked and swirled until her gasps became a scream I had to cover with one hand. She trembled against me, her orgasm ripping through her in the most beautiful way.

When her body relaxed, I peeled my hand from her lips and settled myself between her thighs. She still pulsed as I slid into her, hot and tight and wet.

"Damn," I hissed as I seated myself to the hilt.

She wrapped her legs around me, arching, rolling those hips until I did what she silently demanded.

Flipped us over, to where I was on my back, and she was looking down at me from above.

My fierce woman.

Loved torturing me.

Slowly, agonizingly, she lifted herself until the tip of my cock threatened to slide out.

Then she slammed herself downward, the shock from the sensation sending heat waves of pleasure rolling across my skin.

I reached up, cupping her breasts in my hands, lightly tracing my thumbs over her pert nipples. She arched her head back as she rode me. Her hands roaming over her own body, then lower, to my chest, my neck, anything she could sink her claws too as I pumped her from underneath.

"Oh, God, yes," she moaned, falling forward so that our chests touched.

I gripped her hips, guiding her, keeping pace with how fast and hard she wanted it. Each thrust drawing me closer to my own release. The sight of her, lust-starved and greedy on top of me, pushing me to the brink.

She fisted my hair, jerking it hard enough to bring my mouth to hers. Her tongue swiping in, the flavor of her still in my mouth making her moan even more.

"Fuck," I hissed against her lips as she pushed harder, faster.

"Yes, Warren," she said. "Fucking hell, *yes.*"

"Damn your dirty mouth, woman," I growled, my release soaring through me as I felt her clench around my dick. Another orgasm shaking her body over mine.

I swallowed her moans, kissing her as we came together, my pumps slowing, bringing us down gently.

She loosened her grip on my hair, drawing back when we'd caught our breath.

"I love you," she said, all slick and hot on top of me.

"I fucking love you," I said, smirking.

"You want to go play in a bed now?" She asked, rocking back and forth just enough to make me hiss.

"Hell. Yes." I loved how insatiable she was, how much it matched my own craving for her.

"Then let's go," she said, shifting to stand, gathering the robe that had fallen open around her.

I hopped off the couch, prepared to strip her of that silk so I could watch her walk naked to one of the guestrooms we'd been using over our own. I reached for the silk at her shoulder, but a loud wail stopped me midway.

I dropped my hand, laughing as Jeannine shook her head. "The girl knows," she said. "I swear she *knows.*"

"I'll get her," I said. "You get that sweet ass in bed," I ordered.

"But it's my turn," she argued. "And you have practice tomorrow."

I shrugged. "Which means I won't get to see her or you as much as usual," I said. "I have to get my time in where I can."

"You are everything," she said. "You don't have anything to make up for."

"It's not about that," I whispered, as she followed me toward our bedroom. "It's about me loving my girls."

She swallowed hard, her cheeks flushing as she smiled.

"Now," I said, my hand on our door. I pointed my free hand at the guest bedroom down the hall. "Get that gorgeous ass in there."

"Yes, sir," she said, hurrying down the hall. I watched her beautiful long legs all the way until she turned into the room.

Blinking out of my love-filled-haze, I walked into our room, scooping Katherine up and cradling her against my chest. A few bounces and a whispered *I love you* and she was easily drifting back to sleep.

I didn't put her down right away though.

I held her, gazing at the way she looked like her mother, but had my dark hair. The perfect split between two souls.

"I love you," I whispered. "More than you'll ever know. And I'm going to spend the rest of my life showing you and your mother just how much I do."

Something thick tightened in my throat as I laid her back down, the same thing that seemed to want to burst from my chest.

I never knew happiness like this existed.

Before, hockey had been my one and only love.

And it wasn't until I collided with Nine that I realized how empty hockey was without them by my side.

Now that they were *mine?*

I could finally start living.

The End

THE SEATTLE SHARKS HAVE BITE!

Did you enjoy WINGER? Interested in the Rookie's story? He's skating your way July 25th! Sign up HERE to read his story early!

Sign up here for my newsletter for exclusive content and giveaways!

Follow me on Amazon here to stay up to date on all upcoming releases!

ACKNOWLEDGMENTS

Thank you to my incredible husband and my awesome kids without which I would live a super boring life!

Huge thanks must be paid to these amazing authors who have always offered epic advice and constant support! Not to mention creating insanely hot reads to pass the time with! Sosie Frost, Winter Renshaw, Gina L. Maxwell, and Heather Stone...there aren't enough words for how much I adore each and every one of you!

ABOUT THE AUTHOR

Samantha Whiskey is a wife, mom, lover of her dogs and romance novels. No stranger to hockey, hot alpha males, and a high dose of awkwardness, she tucks herself away to write books her PTA will never know about.

THE CROWN SNEAK PEEK

If you enjoy the Seattle Sharks series, you may enjoy my Modern Day Fairytale Romance series! Turn the page to read the first chapter of THE CROWN!

Xander

How the hell was this happening?

Six months ago I'd been in New York, arguing a human rights case in front of the United Nations. Then the call came, and my entire life turned upside down.

I drew a shaky breath as they slid the last piece of marble in place, effectively sealing my father's coffin in the tomb. It was as if my lungs had simply forgotten how to function since he died almost two weeks ago...as if I didn't know how to breathe in a world where he couldn't.

I was twenty-eight years old and drowning in a sea of regret. Had I learned enough from him? Had I listened when he'd asked? Done as he'd wanted? Why hadn't I spent more time here in the last few years? The cancer had been quick—both a mercy and the worst case scenario, and though he'd told me his soul was ready to leave this life, mine was anything but ready to let him go.

"Your Highness," one of the workers said, tipping his

hat as he walked by. His coworker repeated the gesture. I nodded in acknowledgment, but my powers of speech had apparently left with my oxygen supply.

They were finally all gone. The press, the aristocracy, members of parliament, even my mother and sisters had left with the formal processional. But I needed to see this, needed to stay until he was truly at rest.

"It feels very Game of Thrones down here," Jameson said, sipping from his flask as he came to stand next to me. In age, my twin was only two minutes my junior. In maturity, there was at least a decade between us.

"It's a catacomb. How would you like it to feel?" I asked, reaching for the flask.

"Less like the Middle Ages. Be careful there. It's straight whiskey."

I took a swig and relished the sweet burn as it slid down my throat, warming the chilled numbness that was my torso. "It was built in the Middle Ages, jackass."

He took the flask and threw another swig back. "And one day we'll be buried here, Xander. You, me, Mother, Sophie, Brie, and even your precious Charlotte. This is our future." He spread his arms out and spun slowly as if I needed a tour of the Generations of Wyndhams buried down here. "You will be married to Charlotte, the leader of our people, and I will continue the life of debauchery only the spare to the heir can have."

He was right. No matter how I'd fought this destiny, how badly I didn't want it, *this* was mine—every cold, bleak, practiced and rehearsed moment. Even Charlotte. As much as I loved her like a sister, I'd never wanted more—even if our parents had betrothed us as children. As if Jameson's words had a direct line to my throat, it tightened, and I loosened the knot of my tie.

I was supposed to have another decade or so of freedom. A decade to pursue my passions after I'd finished law school and two subsequent years serving in the Ellestonian military—a hard-won career as an international human rights lawyer. Years to learn from my father after I'd accomplished my own goals, to become the kind of leader he was naturally. But death didn't work on anyone's timeline but his own.

"We need to get up to ground level with the members of our family who still breathe," Jameson said, running a hand through his wreck of a hairdo. He took two steps forward and placed his hand over our father's tomb. "Rest easy, Dad. Xander's got this."

He turned and clapped me on the shoulder as he passed. A moment later I heard his heavy footsteps on the stairs out of the catacomb into the cathedral above us.

I walked to my father's resting place and ran my hand over the smooth marble, my fingers tracing the lines of our family crest.

One by one, I erased the items off my bucket list and tucked them away to the furthest corner of my mind. My hopes of a career, a family that wasn't in the public eye, a wife who wanted me for my heart and not the title behind my name, or because she'd been told it was her legal obligation. I scraped together every selfish thought I could find, and I buried them there with my father.

From now on, my personal wants and needs didn't matter.

"I will make you proud." My voice echoed through the stone structures.

Then I opened my eyes, stood tall, and straightened my tie before turning on my heel to embrace the future I wanted no part in.

I was Alexander Gabriel Edward Wyndham the Fourth, and within the next year, I would be crowned the next King of Elleston and her sixty million people.

Fuck. My. Life.

Xander

Six Months Later

"Alexander, I need to talk to you," Mother hissed in my ear with a smile as she waved to the dignitary from France. Our suite at the Palace was packed to the brim with foreign dignitaries. The cocktail party had been her idea, a way to see everyone in New York City in one event.

"Of course," I said, mirroring her smile. "Did you see that Nicolai is here?" I nodded toward the Prime Minister of Dronovia. He'd gone toe-to-toe with Damian, our Prime Minister more than once. Of course, Damian hadn't given an inch. That man had zero moral flexibility.

"Don't let that tux fool you. He's a shark under that Armani." Her voice was smooth and still sharp, which pretty much described Mom to a T. "Let's find somewhere private."

I cringed but walked her toward the private office. She'd been trying to get me alone all day after she'd heard my address to the United Nations this morning. Maybe I'd gone off on refugee status and humane treatment by EU nations…maybe it had been too much…or not enough.

I opened the door to the office and led my mother in by the small of her back. She was more than a head shorter than my six foot four, but damn if she didn't tower over me when she was pissed. And right now…the woman was livid.

I looked out across the crowd to see Charlotte raise her hand with a small smile. Of course, Mom had made sure Charlotte and her father had been invited to the party. As a Duke in our country, he had every right to be here, but I knew her purpose in New York City was for me, not the UN.

I gave Charlotte a small smile and a nod, then rolled my eyes at my brother, who stood by her side, giving me the god-have-mercy-on-your-soul grimace as Mom entered the office ahead of me.

Mom's smile stayed in place until I closed the door, then promptly fell to a disapproving scowl. "Alexander," she sighed. Her fingers rubbed the small stretch of skin between her eyes.

"Mother," I answered, leaning back against the door. "Are you enjoying our trip? I thought two weeks here might be a little much, but it's a welcome break from the monotony of Elleston, isn't it?" Any topic of conversation was preferable to what she was going to throw at me.

Her sharp blue eyes could have cut a hole through my head. I missed her smile. The one she had before Dad died. The one she shared with Jameson, ever the rogue with his dark, constantly messed up hair. Mine was always respectably tamed. Though we were identical, it was as if our styles had taken on aspects of our personality—mine always within the limits of propriety, and Jameson's as wild as he was. And though our Mother expected me to be the epitome of every etiquette class, she loved Jameson more for that wildness he was allowed to keep.

"Enough. Alexander, it's been almost six months since your father passed—"

"I'm well aware."

"And though I don't mind being Queen Regent, you can't be crowned until you're married. That's clear in our Constitution—"

"Which is *clearly* outdated."

"That's not up for debate. The women must stop. Charlotte knows what's expected of her, and it's not like you two don't get along fabulously."

"As friends," I said softly. "And it's not like I have women in and out of the palace like Jameson does." I liked women. Hell, I loved women. I just had more respect for them than allowing anyone I spent the night with to be the subject of tabloid speculation. There was such a thing as discretion.

"Jameson is not the heir."

"And there you have it."

"Alexander, what you have with Charlotte is real. Friendship can be the base for an amazing marriage," she answered, her eyes pleading. "If you'll just announce that you're engaged, that will appease Parliament for the meantime. A short engagement, and then we'll crown you the day after the wedding if need be. It's not like the plans aren't already in motion, anyway."

"And if I want love? Or at least passion?"

"You love Charlotte, I have seen how you care for each other."

"Like a sister," I responded with a little bite. "We've

never even *dated*. We both agreed to date other people as we wanted until the time came."

"Well, the time has come, and royal marriages have been made of less. You love her, and you'll be passionate about your country. That's far more than some have had."

"Far more than *you* had?"

She blinked, then patted back an imaginary strand of her salt and pepper hair. "I was lucky to love your father. It is my deepest hope that you'll find the same happiness in your marriage. But if not...then duty before all else."

"I am twenty-eight, and I'm still learning everything I need to rule this country. Now isn't the best time to throw a marriage into the mix."

The noise of the party behind us made our silence all the more poignant.

Mother smoothed her designer gown, and then looked up at me with a calm determination. "I give you three months to announce your engagement, or I'll do it for you. That's the longest we can wait before we flirt with the constitutional deadline. Already, there are cries to disband the monarchy, and we must show that you are ready for the role of King, which according to our laws, means marriage. The time for...play has passed, and though I know this was never the path you wanted, this is the path you'll take."

I stepped aside, and she swept through the door like the queen she was, regal and composed. I knew she suffered under that carefully placed mask, knew how much she missed my father, but she never showed the outside world her pain.

Before I could swing the door shut, Charlotte glided in, her pink gown elegant against her pale skin and dark brown hair. She was a classic beauty, but what made her even more breathtaking was the heart she had to match.

"Hey," she said softly, shutting the door behind her. "You okay?"

"Yeah," I said, making my way to the rolling bar in the corner. I poured myself a finger of whatever was in the amber container and took a sniff. Brandy. A little too hoity for my tastes, but there wasn't a beer in sight.

"What's going on, Xan?" Charlotte leaned a hip against the back of the winged chair that faced a desk.

"We're supposed to announce our engagement in three months." I said it with all the excitement of a trip to the guillotine.

"Oh," she whispered, standing up straight. "Are you ready for that?"

"Do you *want* that?" I fired back.

She glanced away, then brought her green eyes back to meet mine. "I want whatever you need."

"Jesus, Charlotte. You deserve more than this. Than a guy who sees you as a sister. Don't you want more?" She had to want more because I sure as hell did.

She bit her lower lip. "I've been told since I was five that we would marry. That I would help you rule our country. I gave up on romantic love years ago."

"That's sad. I love our country, too. I'm ready to King, but this is an asinine law." I raised the glass to my lips but was interrupted when Jameson walked in.

"So this is where the party went." His eyes flickered to Charlotte, who rolled hers. "What's wrong, Charlie? Did I interrupt anything important?"

"Don't call me that," she seethed.

I tried to hide my smile and failed. Jameson was the only one who ever ruffled Charlotte's feathers. In fact, I was pretty sure he poked at her just to see the biggest reaction he could get. The pair had been at each other's throats since we were kids.

"You look like you need to get out of here," Jameson said, his eyes narrowing in my direction.

"I would in a heartbeat." A heartbeat. That's what a three-month deadline felt like.

Jameson produced a set of keys. "Take her."

"For fuck's sake, did you buy another car?" I asked, examining the Maserati key.

"Yeah."

"Like you needed one here in New York?"

"It was green," he said with a shrug as if that was the only reasoning he needed.

"Go," Charlotte said quietly. "We'll cover for you. Just get out of here and breathe a little, Xander." She stepped closer and leaned up to whisper. "And be happy. No matter what is expected of us, I want you to be happy, and if that means we shake up the plans others made for us, so be it."

"Charlotte..." I whispered, aware that she was telling me she was willing to walk away from our parents' arrangement.

"You're right. I love you like a brother, and there's a future coming for us that is...well, asinine. Go find some happy."

I kissed her on the forehead and strode out of the room, my steps eating up the distance quickly. Jameson ran ahead of me, knocking over an entire tray of champagne flutes, and I slipped out while security rushed to help him. They were preoccupied keeping people out, not *in*.

A quick trip to the valet and I was behind the wheel of Jameson's new Maserati, which I noticed was the same color of Charlotte's eyes. I made it out of the city in good time and headed north.

Where the hell was I going? Unlike my perfectly planned out life, I had no destination in mind. I rolled down the window and was hit with a blast of freezing January air. Ripping off my tie, I turned the music up and settled into the soft leather. I had a full tank of gas, so did it matter if I didn't have a destination? I had no obligations for the next couple of days. Letting my mind wander, I let the car put as many miles between me and my fate as I could.

Ruling Elleston was something I could do. I'd been raised to the role, trained, educated and prepared in every way possible. But marrying Charlotte? Sharing my life—my bed—with someone I couldn't picture sexually?

How the hell was I going to do that?

I liked sex. Scratch that. I fucking *loved* sex. Every nuance of it, from the tastes, the sounds, the consuming pleasure—it all added up to phenomenal. I'd never cheat on Charlotte once were married—hell, once we were actually *together*—engaged. But I wasn't sure I could fuck her, either.

I drove for hours, and then the first snowflakes hit the windshield.

Slowing, I watched in fascination as the sky went from crystal clear to blinding white. I'd heard storms moved in fast in this part of the country, but *damn*.

Another twenty minutes north and the roads were covered. The snow rose high on either side of the highway—this region was no stranger to the fluffy white stuff.

"Shit," I muttered to myself. It was time to turn back, or at least find a hotel for the night. I pulled off the highway at the nearest exit and went to loop back to get on the South-bound side...but there wasn't one.

"You seriously pulled off at the only fucking exit in Upstate New York that doesn't have a return?" I asked myself. Fumbling with my phone, I cursed when I saw it was down to one percent.

I committed as many of the directions to the next on ramp as I could to memory and wound the Maserati through the forested, hilly curves of the Catskills. I slid a few times, but it was nothing I couldn't handle. But if this kept up, the depth was going to be an issue.

I glanced at the road sign telling me the next onramp was in one mile. When I looked back to the road, a deer bounded out of the forest and onto the street.

"Shit!" I shouted, slamming on the breaks. The car slid, and I downshifted, trying to turn away from the animal. I missed the massive buck by only a few feet, sliding off the road, and into a snowbank.

The car slammed to a halt, and the seatbelt stopped my forward momentum with a snap, but not before my head hit something as the airbag deployed.

A fine powder filled the car from the airbag, and I threw open the door, coughing as I stepped into the night. I felt a warm trickle and pulled my fingers from my forehead to find a light stream of blood. *Great.*

Leaning back into the car, I grabbed my phone.

The fucking thing was dead.

"This is what impulsivity gets you," I muttered.

The car was buried in the bank past the first set of tires, and the back had no traction on the snow-covered ground. There was zero chance I was getting it out of there.

"Couldn't buy an SUV, could you?" I cursed my brother instead of my own stupidity. I was in nothing but a tux and dress shoes, about to walk a mile in sub-zero temperatures to the highway and pray that someone stopped.

At least it would make for an interesting story.

I put my hands in my pockets and started walking down

the side of the road, ignoring the cold that seeped through my dress clothes and shoes. As I passed a smaller road, I looked up the hill and saw lights through the blowing snow. That was my best bet if I didn't want to freeze to death.

I trudged up the hill, thanking God that I didn't fall on my ass.

The house was white, with lights streaming out from the glassed-in wrap around porch. More than the appearance, I cared about the smoke billowing from the chimney. They had heat.

Correction. *She* had heat.

I paused, the snow up to my knees on what I assumed was her sidewalk. She was beautiful. Her wide, blue eyes narrowed as she looked out over the snow through her window. She was petite, but perfectly curved—from what I could see—her blonde hair falling just around her shoulders. As she brushed it back, I caught the color underneath. Pink. It was pink. No...purple. Holy shit, the underlayer of her hair was dyed like a unicorn. More than beautiful, she was exquisite. Maybe I was going into hypothermia because she had to be a hallucination.

But I desperately needed her to be real.

I stumbled up the steps, having lost the majority of feeling in my feet, and rang the bell.

"Please be real."

WANT THE REST OF XANDER'S STORY?

Check out The Crown here!
It's only $0.99 or FREE in Kindle Unlimited!

18078182R00134